Caroline b Cooney

Family Reunion

mammoth

First published in the USA 1989
by Bantam Books, a division of
Bantam Doubleday Dell Publishing Group, Inc
First published in Great Britain 1991
by Teens Mandarin
Reissued 1997 by Mammoth
an imprint of Reed International Books Ltd
Michelin House, 81 Fulham Road, London SW3 6RB
and Auckland and Melbourne

Copyright © 1989 by Caroline B Cooney

The moral rights of the author have been asserted.

ISBN 0 7497 0533 7

10 9 8 7 6 5 4 3 2 1

A CIP catalogue record for this title
is available from the British Library

Printed and bound in Great Britain
by Cox & Wyman Ltd, Reading, Berkshire

Chapter 1

*I*t began when we found out that our new summer house had an old bomb shelter in the backyard, and my brother, Angus, decided to sell condominium time-shares in it. Angus is twelve and a terrific salesman. He used to sell my Girl Scout cookies and calendars for me, and not once did a customer ask why a boy with a crew cut was in the Girl Scouts. He has red hair and freckles, and I think there is something about red hair and freckles that makes strangers relax their defenses, and buy, buy, buy.

Soon after we examined our bomb shelter, Angus divided the year into fifty-two weeks and went off to sell ten shares per week of year-round, lifetime, come-as-you-are survival shelter use.

It was that "come-as-you-are" line that people liked. You could tell it soothed them to know that when the bomb fell, they didn't have to dress up to take advantage of their time-share.

I said, "But Angus. What if the bomb falls in

September, and somebody bought a lifetime, first-week-in-March use?"

Angus drew a long, slow, sad finger across his throat. "Poor planning," he told me. "People have to think ahead. Know their global politics." He turned to his latest potential buyer, an innocent Vermont child with an untouched allowance. "Or better yet," Angus said joyfully, "buy a share in each week of the year! That way you'll never have a worry."

Before Daddy found out and stopped him, Angus had sold seventy-two shares. Angus even had a computer program worked out for dividing each shareholder's right to the cans of Campbell's soup that were in there, too. (Although I personally would be worried about chicken noodle soup from 1958.)

Daddy went berserk.

"We bought this summer house because you were going to enjoy fresh air! Swim in the lake, fish for trout, climb every mountain. People said that children need a backyard for a normal, stable upbringing, and so I said, okay. June through August they'll have a backyard. I'll make these kids stable if it kills me. So what happens? You come up here from New York City, demoralize all these nice Vermont kids, rip off their allowances, and sell them—"

Daddy paused. He was praying Angus would admit he hadn't really sold time-shares to a bomb shelter; he had really gotten all that money from a paper route.

"Dad, it's a new idea," said Angus proudly. "A fresh concept. I bet nobody else in Vermont is doing it."

Daddy got a grip on himself and asked what Angus had been charging.

"Five dollars a share, Dad. It's a bargain. Everybody saw that right off."

Family
Reunion

My father is a large man—well over six feet, with shoulders like a yardstick. Whenever he has to deal with Angus he takes very deep breaths, so his chest rises, and his suit jacket lifts, and his tie swings free. It's like watching a rocket preparing for launch. You're always a bit worried about the explosion. "Angus," said my father, "we have hardly arrived in this town. So far I know the guy who pumps my gas, the mailman, and the short-order cook at the coffee shop."

"Gee, Dad, that's a shame. I've met everybody. I've been going door-to-door for days."

Daddy's chest sank back to resting position. He looked up at the ceiling, which in the summer house is quite close to his head, and he frequently communes with the cracks there. Then he stared at his sweet-faced, freckled son and said that he had just remembered pressing business back in New York City. He'd be gone for weeks now. Possibly all summer. That it was up to Angus and me and Annette (our stepmother) to go door-to-door, return all the money, and apologize for Angus being such a sick puppy that he would even think of selling bomb shares.

Angus had, after all, earned three hundred sixty dollars, and the thought of giving it back was not a happy one. He put on the expression of a puppy at the pound, entreating us to give him love and affection. Earnestly he explained that this sort of thing would look really great on a college application.

Daddy said this kind of thing would make any reasonable college admissions office bar the door.

Angus said he thought he would write Grandma about it, because Grandma was always proud of him, even if nobody else was.

Daddy said if Angus went and told Grandma, Daddy

3

would kill him. Daddy's chest began to expand alarmingly. Angus backed up a bit.

I backed up completely and said I would go check the mail.

Mail is the best thing about having a summer house in Vermont. The big black mailbox pokes up out of tall white daisies and high grassy weeds on the other side of a narrow country road, and when the little red flag is down, you know somebody has written you.

Vermont is entirely treed. You'd think they had a genuine fear of meadows, open spaces, and views. Trees curve in over the roads and houses and towns, wave upon wave, as if local zoning laws require you to live in a green aquarium. Only the lake, being filled with water, is barren of trees.

I walked through the filtered sun and pulled down the little curved door of the black mailbox.

The only mail was a letter from Aunt Maggie.

Aunt Maggie is Daddy's older sister. She lives out in the Midwest, where she and her family lead A Perfect Life. We call them The Perfects, because it's rather like their real last name, which is Preffyn. In the old days, when we were sort of perfect ourselves, we used to visit them, but we don't anymore. Daddy says he doesn't have the energy.

Aunt Maggie married Uncle Todd, and she is lovely and he is handsome, and she is chairman of the school board and he is a pharmacist. They have a backyard, of course, have always had a backyard, and therefore their children, Brett and Carolyn, are also Perfect. Brett is sixteen and handsome and Carolyn is fourteen and beautiful. They were never awkward and fat, never had braces, never had pimples, and never got anything below a B plus. In gym they are always chosen first for teams. That is just the kind of family they are.

4

When they visit us in New York City, we like to walk down the sidewalk and point to perfectly innocent people waiting for the bus and whisper, "Careful—drug deal." Carolyn and Brett always fall for this, and tell their mother, and Aunt Maggie says if we just had a backyard to play in, we would be stable, like her kids.

Stable is a big word in Aunt Maggie's life. She has stability, Carolyn and Brett have tremendous stability, but we have none. We are unstable, unbalanced, and at risk.

She loves that one: *at risk.*

As if my brother and sister and I are poised at the edge of a cliff, teetering dangerously, nobody within reach to pull us away from a smushed-to-slush death.

When we were younger, you see, our mother fell in love with a dashing, romantic, handsome French newspaper reporter who was at that time covering the United Nations for a Paris paper. Mother left Daddy and went to live with Jean-Paul, and a few years later they went on to Paris.

We stayed with Daddy. This was partly because we wanted to stay with Daddy, and partly because Mother wasn't sure we would fit in with her new lifestyle anyway. Although we could agree that Angus wouldn't fit easily into anybody's lifestyle, my sister Joanna and I did not like hearing that we wouldn't either.

Joanna, who is the oldest, is spending her entire summer with Mother and Jean-Paul; she is the first of us to visit France. Joanna left the very afternoon that school ended—June 17—and won't be back till school starts again—September 8.

Daddy likes us to write to Mother.

We have a bad attitude toward doing this, especially since Mother doesn't write back, she telephones.

5

A few weeks ago, I wrote that Angus was enjoying his new leg.

Mother telephoned, horrified, demanding to know what had happened to Angus's old leg. Angus said it had gotten all crushed and thrown in the dump, but he had gotten a new one cheap, and Mother wasn't to worry about the bill.

Mother telephoned Daddy at work in New York City for details. (It is hard to say which of them hates these phone calls more.) Of course Daddy didn't know Angus had any fake legs, let alone cheap ones, so it was just the sort of conversation that made Mother abandon Daddy in the first place. Mother called back to Vermont and demanded to speak to Annette about the leg, but Annette is afraid of Mother, and whispered to Angus to say she wasn't home, and Angus of course said, "Annette says to tell you she's not home."

By then I don't think Mother really cared about Angus's leg. I think she called Daddy in New York again just to be difficult. This time Daddy remembered that Angus likes to use an old hollow detachable mannequin's leg as a briefcase, or tote bag, and he was ready with a sane, reasonable explanation for Mother. Mother did not think anybody in the picture was being either sane or reasonable.

But that was the past. Nobody cared about Angus's leg any more. We just wanted to take the pressure off the bomb-share deals, so I ran into the house to read Aunt Maggie's letter aloud.

My father had sunk into the only chair in the summer house large enough to support him. Summer house furniture turned out to be quite flimsy, but Annette doesn't mind, as this means she gets to redecorate and replace it all.

The house in Vermont has no curtains on any of the downstairs windows. By day the sun moves slowly from one pane of glass to the next. Hot little squares of sun lie first on the living room floor, slide to the table, drift into the next room and become late afternoon slants across the kitchen counters.

The summer heat was already vanishing, and Daddy had yanked off his tie, tossed his jacket over a chairback, and was closing his eyes. The afghan on the back of the easy chair was pale blue with pink flower trim. It sank down when Daddy did and lay on his shoulders like a baby blanket on a grizzly bear.

I said, "You want to hear a letter from Aunt Maggie?" I didn't give anybody a choice. I read, " 'Dear Brother Charlie.' "

Daddy said that made him sound like an inmate at an institution for adult mentally handicapped. We did not tell him he also looked like one, what with the baby blanket scooched around his cheeks.

" 'It is hard to believe, but Todd and I are approaching our twentieth wedding anniversary!!!!!!!!' " I went on.

Eight exclamation points. Enough to make anybody gag, but especially Daddy, who did not reach a first anniversary on Wife Number One, hit a twelfth with Wife Number Two (our mother), and is barely within reach of a second on Wife Number Three (Annette).

"Don't worry, Dad," Angus consoled him. "All those exclamation points mean Aunt Maggie is as surprised as anybody that it lasted all those years."

" 'And of course,' " I quoted on, " 'we want to have a big and wonderful family celebration of this unique event.' "

"Notice how she's rubbing in how unique it is," said Daddy.

I kept reading. " 'So we've planned a family re-union gala for August!' "

My aunt Maggie is known for her great enthusiasms, which tend to tire out everybody but Aunt Maggie. Now even her handwriting was bigger and more excited. I made a note to get a library book on how to analyze handwriting because I was sure there were depths to plumb in Aunt Maggie's.

" 'We're even getting in touch with old friends from high school, Charlie!!!!! We'll want everybody to come!! Joanna must fly back from Paris and this will be our chance to get to know dear Annette at last, and how wonderful it will be for Shelley and Angus to be back in Barrington again!!!!' "

"Where they have all those backyards," said Angus.

Annette looked as if she would rather postpone meeting The Perfects for another hundred years or so. In her situation I would certainly feel the same, since Annette does not measure up to anybody, especially Wife Number Two (Mother) and Aunt Maggie. Annette began playing with Angus's Queen Anne's lace. Angus read that you could dye Queen Anne's lace, so he has bunches sitting in glasses of water and food coloring. Nothing has happened with yellow and green, but red and blue have promise; they are now a sick pastel instead of white. Annette shifted Queen Anne's lace glasses all over the table.

"Can I telephone Joanna and tell her about the family reunion?" I begged. "Please, please?"

Daddy looked wary. He likes talking to Joanna, but he's afraid Mother will be home and he'll have to talk to her, or worse, that Jean-Paul will be home and

8

they'll have to have a civilized conversation. The crummy thing about divorce and remarriage is how you're required to be civilized about it, and not scream ugly things, especially when several years have gone by and if you have any stability at all, you have gotten over it.

"I'll tell Joanna you're not home," I said kindly.

I didn't get the usual lecture on How Expensive It Is To Telephone Across The Atlantic Ocean, nor even the secondary lecture on You Should Write More Letters Instead. Daddy was weak from dealing with Angus and didn't even remember to tell me to set the timer so I wouldn't talk more than fifteen minutes.

Annette remembered. I think that is probably a stepmother's role in life, remembering the toll-call timer.

I ran upstairs to my bedroom.

Vacation bedrooms are different from real bedrooms. In New York, my half of the room is lined with shelves and cabinets. Each shelf has a front and a back layer of books, cassettes, games I used to play, dolls I used to collect, papers I wrote last year. The drawers are stuffed with sweaters and sweatshirts, and socks pop out when you tug them open. My view is limited to Joanna's side of the room, which is even more cluttered because she's had more years to clutter in. There is no visible wallpaper because we've been taping up posters for years, without ever taking the first ones down, so that formerly adored stars have only their feet showing beneath the hair of the currently adored rock stars, who are partially obscured by the perfume advertisements Jo cuts from magazines and the cartoons I cut from the newspaper.

In Vermont my room is utterly bare. It has a gleaming wooden floor, white walls, and nothing of me except my clothing, hidden in closet and bureau. The

9

view through two narrow windows, curtained with white, flower-sprigged muslin, is the treetops shading the mail-box. The leaves are never quiet. They shift, as if they are straining to see more. In a high wind the leaves run in place, like basketball players who finally get off the bench and into the game.

I sat cross-legged on the bed and dialed the twelve digits to reach Joanna. I love dialing direct to France; I feel so sophisticated.

I have this terrible fear that Joanna will fit per-fectly in Mother and Jean-Paul's lifestyle and that she will stay there forever and not come home in September.

Every time I talk to her, and she's bubbling away about staying in kings' castles, and eating dinner at ten P.M., and strolling around Paris eating real croissants (as opposed to the shabby make-believe ones we eat in New York), I feel as if I am losing her. Joanna and I don't share a bedroom anymore, and she hasn't seen the bomb shelter, and she hasn't lived in the summer house, and she didn't help Angus with the computer program for Campbell's soup, and she probably thinks it's more fun in France, and will probably vanish like Mother.

So actually Aunt Maggie's Perfection was good tim-ing. Joanna would have to come home in August and we would all get very stable from all those Barrington backyards and Joanna would stay in our family after all.

But when I read Aunt Maggie's letter out loud to her, Joanna said, "Mid-August?" in a distracted voice. "Impossible, Shelley. Out of the question. Simply can-not make it. Jean-Paul and Mother and I will be in England. We have our theater tickets in London all arranged."

10

I plucked at the telephone cord as if it were a guitar string. Outside the chorus of insects picked up and rasped as if planning an assault on the bedroom window. "You'd rather go to theater in London than have a watermelon-seed-spitting contest with Brett and Carolyn?" I said to my sister.

Joanna laughed. "That was three years ago. Only Angus is enough of a baby to do that now. You're going to be so jealous of me, Shell. While you're escorting Annette in among The Perfects, I shall be walking down the aisle where Diana married Prince Charles, or standing where Lady Jane Grey was executed."

"Daddy will make you come," I said, knowing he would not.

"He can't. It's Mother's time."

In divorce you cannot trespass on the other parent's time. It's a rule. Of course you do, all the time, but you do it quietly and sneakily. I said, "Oh, just skip London."

"Nope. I've been to Barrington. I've never been to London." Joanna changed the subject quickly, because I am very good at making people feel guilty. I am as good at that as Angus is at selling Girl Scout cookies. Once my mother said she needed the Atlantic Ocean between us because of all the guilt I lay on her if she's closer.

"But Jo, you have to come!" I cried. "I need you. Angus needs you."

"Nonsense. You guys will be fine. Just leave Annette at home. She'll embarrass you if you bring her."

I could not think of any easy way to leave my stepmother at home. "Lock her in a closet with enough water to last her a week?" I said.

Joanna felt I should give this serious thought. She

11

believed that Daddy's standards had fallen over the years. "Mother is incredibly more intelligent, beautiful, interesting, and bilingual than Annette," she said.

"Annette is hardly even one-lingual," I told her. "Especially after Angus has worked her over." I told Joanna about the bomb shares.

Joanna laughed for an entire two minutes of expensive transatlantic phone call. She has such a wonderful laugh, all loud and boisterous and room-filling. It hurt to listen to her laugh and not have her in the room with me. Which would I rather have? I thought. A room here all to myself, with privacy and quiet and bare walls? Or Joanna sharing, getting ready for dates, eating cookies and getting crumbs on my bed (she's never dumb enough to eat Oreos on her bed) and borrowing my earrings?

No contest.

"Oooooh," Joanna whispered suddenly. "I just thought of something, Shelley. You know who else you might meet at a big reunion where they're even inviting Daddy's old high school friends? I bet you'll finally meet Wife Number One! Celeste."

I have always been terribly grateful to Celeste for preferring her career in Chicago over Daddy, because if she hadn't, we would not have been born. I think my father is perfect, and I cannot understand how Celeste, who knew him when he was so young and handsome, could have thought anything different. But it's just as well she did.

"I always used to think," said Joanna, her voice dreamily crossing two thousand miles of choppy blue ocean, "that Daddy and Celeste had a son they never told us about. A boy a few years older than me. And somehow I would meet him, all unknowing, and we

12

would fall in love and date, and I would end up marrying my half brother."

"Eeeeuuuhhhh!" I screamed. "How disgusting! Joanna, how can you even think of things like that? You know they didn't have any children."

"We know they didn't *tell* us if they had any," Joanna corrected me.

It was so thrilling and repelling to think about. A hidden, secret brother or sister.

The timer went off with a loud ding that Annette could hear all the way downstairs in the kitchen, so there was no pretending it hadn't sounded. "Oh, no," wailed Joanna, hearing it in France, too. "We didn't get to the important things yet."

"Like whether you're coming!" I cried.

"No, I'm not coming. You think I want to hang around in Barrington wringing the sweat out of my T-shirt on some deadly hot August afternoon while everybody tells Daddy how unstable we are? Forget it, little sister. You're on your own."

Chapter 2

*P*art of Daddy's stability program is fresh air, so Saturday morning, he took us on a hike at the state park, and we had a picnic at a famous Revolutionary War battle site. Then we picked our own sweet corn at a farm where you can also pick your own zucchini, but even Daddy was against that. Just when we thought we had had enough fresh air, we rented bicycles and peddled uphill and down. Sunday we toured famous historical houses and noticed how small the beds were and had the usual Early American House discussion on whether people were short back then or just slept all curled up.

Everybody was quite relieved when Daddy went back to New York City before dawn on Monday morning. His heart, he claimed, could not take the combination of Angus and all this rural green serenity. Our hearts were rather tired also, and we watched television all Monday, as an antidote to so much fresh air.

Annette didn't know what to do. This is frequently

the case with Annette, which is kind of nice in a step-mother, because you can push her around so easily. How could she face people in this town? Her very first conversation would have to be about bomb shares.

"I wish you'd stop calling it a bomb share," said Angus. "I didn't sell a single person a share in a bomb. I sold them shares in a bomb *shelter*."

Annette said she thought *I* looked like the kind of person who would be good at returning shares to strangers who would probably get mad.

I have never been able to decide what I look like. I think I have potential. But I'm not there yet. When I look in the mirror I see a very unfinished product. (Joanna says there is no such thing as a "finished" fourteen-year-old anyhow.)

It's funny. I cannot do anything if I have to do it alone. But with a companion at my side—even a nut-case brother like Angus—I can take on the world. Or at least Vermont.

One way or another, you meet a lot of people through Angus. All Vermont wanted to stop and chat and find out if Angus did this sort of thing routinely. Angus would lean on his leg, which he uses as a walking stick when he's in the mood, and fish five dollars out of the hollow that runs from the mannequin's thigh to its toe, and solemnly hand it over.

You had your stock reactions to this. People who fled and people who started laughing.

There was one house where grandfather, father, and son were all named DeWitt, which appeared to be a first name. I narrowed my eyes at the DeWitt who was about my own age, and wondered what it was like to be saddled with three generations of that ghastly name. Angus was returning five dollars to DeWitt's little sister, Veronica. DeWitt said they'd only give the five dollars back if they got a bomb-shelter tour. After I convinced Angus that no, he could not charge extra for the bomb-shelter tour, DeWitt and Veronica fell in line behind us.

Eventually we had collected quite a parade, patiently waiting in front yards while Angus and I went up the steps to return five dollars to the next victim. Some of the victims were edgy about opening the door under the circumstances, so Angus hollered loud enough to do two houses at a time, and everybody in his parade clapped.

By the end of the week I felt as if we had lived in Vermont for years and I am sure Vermont felt the same.

Annette steered clear of the village and all adults who might find out that she was responsible for the behavior of the kid with the leg and the bomb shelter. She did things like make grape jam, which we had known you could do, but had not known you could do *yourself*. We really got into it, stirring and sugaring and filling the cute little jelly jars, with their flat lids and separate screwtops.

But when it was time to have peanut butter and jelly, Angus opted for Kraft. He knew what was in it, he explained. He trusted it.

DeWitt and Veronica came in their rowboat and took us to their house around the far side of the lake so we could watch old rented James Bond movies. Angus felt they should have an outboard motor on their boat, as oars were too tedious. DeWitt said *sssshhhhh,* because his grandfather DeWitt was at that very moment trying to stop the Noise Pollution On The Lake perpetrated by people with outboard motors.

On Friday, Daddy came up from the city with a huge bag of goodies from Zabar's, which is my favorite delicatessen in the world. I am sure shopping at Zabar's on a regular basis makes you just as stable as all the backyards in Barrington. We had wonderful bread and bagels and cheesecakes and chocolate all weekend long. When Daddy was very relaxed and having yet another fat slice of bread slathered with Vermont butter and Annette's grape jam, Angus explained that not everybody wanted his five dollars back.

My father was suspicious. You get that way when you live with Angus.

"It's true," said Annette. "We had six who would rather keep their lifetime use of the bomb shelter."

We? I thought. I looked hard at Annette but she did not own up to having stayed safely indoors during the entire bomb-shelter-return time span.

"Probably going to rent it out to skiers in February," muttered my father. "I can see the newspaper ad now. 'Unique accommodation—cozy underground space—' "

Angus thought this was possibly the most brilliant idea our father had ever had. "And here I thought you were some dull businessman in New York," said Angus wonderingly, offering to shake Daddy's hand. "We'd better put the ad in the paper now, Dad. People will be wanting to make their winter plans."

My father stared out the window into the dark. In Vermont after the sun vanishes, the grass goes black, and the trees and lake turn indigo, like blue-stained shadows, but the sky is translucent. You can see through

17

its holes to the stars, as if the night were an old skirt with a silver slip. "Maybe when we go to Barrington, they'll keep Angus," Daddy said.

Annette said that from what we had told her of Barrington, they did not grow people like Angus there.

"New blood," said my father hopefully. "They need an infusion of—"

"I'm old blood, Dad," said Angus. "I'm practically a native of that town."

"You've been there three times," said our father. He threatened Angus with bodily mutilation if Angus brought up the ski rental idea again. He said Angus would resemble that damn leg he carried around—severed at important junctions of his body. Annette said nervously that was just the sort of talk we must be sure to avoid around The Perfects.

I have always wanted to be part of a big family. I used to think if we had just stayed in Barrington, or if we were Wife Number One's children and Daddy never reached Two and Three, then we would have stayed in Barrington and my cousin Carolyn and I would hang out together.

I wondered what Brett and Carolyn did all day long in Barrington. It's a pretty town. It's flat, which is nice for biking and skateboarding. Huge oaks and maples divide the wide front yards and there are bushes as big as bunk beds for when you're playing hide-and-seek. Barrington River is too swift to swim in, but there are town pools and a shopping mall, a pretty little downtown and a brick elementary school, like the ones in picture books.

Carolyn and Brett have rope swings and a hammock, an old tire swing and a sandbox. I remember

18

those from the visit when I was eleven and Mommy and Daddy were divorcing and everybody was saying how terrible it was, and it *was* terrible. I sat in Grandma's lap and cried, and she had a big white wicker rocking chair and we rocked and rocked.

My grandparents used to live in a house just like DeWitt's, with brown shingles and big porches. The porch ceiling was painted light blue, like a morning sky, and the floor was painted gray, and everything was peeling. Once on a rainy day we roller-skated for hours, wearing dents in the porch, but Grandma just smiled and made more lemonade. I always think of Barrington like that. It's always summer, and we're always drinking lemonade, and Grandma is always giving me a hug.

But Grandpa died, and Grandma moved to Arizona to get away from the harsh winters. Somebody bought their house and put yellow aluminum siding over the shingles and took off one of the porches and added skylights and it's a whole different house. The one time I saw it, I had to look away, because I was afraid of losing the memory of the brown house where Grandpa lived and Grandma hugged me and Mommy and Daddy were still married.

We sat quietly while Daddy had his iced tea and Angus and I had ripe red cherries from the bowl Annette had put on the table among the pastel Queen Anne's lace. I love fresh fruit. Angus and I collected the pits in a cup he had made from painting the bottom of a liter soda bottle. Angus was going to plant his in the gutter around the roof, to see if they would take root in the rotting maple leaves Daddy had not yet cleaned out. I planned to offer mine to the crow I was trying to tame.

19

I'm fourteen, I thought. Do normal fourteen-year-old girls save their cherry pits? Do they get all excited about dialing extra digits on a phone call? Do they have brothers with extra legs?

I imagined the reunion. The Perfects all lined up—clean and stable and calm, ready for the camera. Their clothes would probably match and might even be ironed. Everybody would have had a haircut yesterday.

We'd be a shambles. Angus waving his leg and Annette being dull. Daddy looking like an illustration for the three bears, and me trying to herd my family into place, like a little sheepdog.

"Did you sign up for the library summer reading program?" asked our father. He probably figured any children's activity at a Vermont library had to be safe.

"Yes!" cried Angus, with whom nothing is safe. "They're doing unusual pets. Mine will win all the prizes."

It is always Angus's intention to win all the prizes. He gets one now and then, usually from a science teacher who is praying he will go away.

I was not in the summer reading program. The librarian said I was too old. He waved me away from the safe little shelf of Young Adult books and shooed me into the Real Adult books. I don't like Real Adult books. Actually I still like Carolyn Heywood and Beverly Cleary and anybody else who writes nice, homey, safe stories, but although Angus is brave enough to carry a leg with money stuffed down it, I am not brave enough to check out third-grade readers.

The library here has only two rooms: children and

grown-ups divided by the circulation desk. The children's room is old and soft, with dark wooden walls and old wooden tables. You can squat on the picture book bench and read a Berenstain Bears with your left hand while your right hand picks out a nice mystery from the YA collection. The adult reading table has *The Wall Street Journal.* Anybody knows which makes better reading.

Angus brought from the basement a box he had constructed of five cookie sheets and one windowpane soldered together. It was rickety, with a sideways list like a ship about to sink. "Look," he whispered. Through the glass wall of the box you could see two little dark things racing around.

"Cockroaches!" screamed Annette.

Angus beamed at her. "Good for you," he complimented her. "They're very smart, you know. When the world ends, they won't. They've been here since dinosaurs. The librarian said that was very clever of me, bringing my own cockroaches from home." Angus stared admiringly into his shaky box.

Annette yelled that we didn't have any cockroaches in either of our homes. She wanted to know how she could even enter the library now to borrow a simple romance when the librarian thought our house was full of cockroaches and the other patrons thought we routinely sold shares in bomb shelters.

Angus waved away her distress and told us all about the librarian, a neat guy who really believed that Angus would be able to train his cockroaches to run down the walkways made of shoebox that Angus had put inside the cookie-sheet container.

Daddy said he felt tired and if the cockroaches

19696
FICTION

were secured for the night, he would just go lie down. Annette said she didn't care how secure the cockroaches were—either the cockroaches were leaving the house this instant or she was.

Of course any stepchild worth his red blood likes that kind of threat from a stepmother.

Angus and I really got into the idea of Annette leaving and the roaches staying, which led Daddy to take Annette out for a late dinner, and Angus and I had to stay home and have toasted-cheese sandwiches. This was not enough supper, so we had cold cereal with bananas, too, and that wasn't enough, so we defrosted a Pepperidge Farm cake and split that. Then we had had enough.

Monday Daddy went back to New York City again.

Angus agreed to keep the cockroaches at the library and the librarian told Annette that in spite of everything, she could go on borrowing books because it is a free country.

Annette said she would rather be welcomed on the basis of being a nice person rather than because of a constitutional requirement, but at least she had plenty to read.

Joanna's next letter was very firm.

Dear Shell,
I have rules for you. Promise me you'll keep them at the reunion. First, stick up for Mother. Don't let them say anything bad about her. Real mothers don't give up custody and Aunt Maggie is bound to harp on that. Harp right back.

Now, don't let them say anything bad about Daddy, either. That will be tricky because they'll certainly want to say something bad about somebody. Get them started saying bad things about Annette; that should keep everybody busy for a few weeks. I'm so glad I'll be having an adventure in England instead. I'll be spared all that talk about what hard lives we've led and how remarkable that we've come through it all so well.

Barrington is going to be a zoo. Enjoy, little sister. What do you want me to bring you from London?

Love, Joanna.

DeWitt and Veronica began showing up rather frequently. All I had to do was sit on the edge of our dock with my toes in the water and DeWitt and his little sister would appear in one of their boats. It was rather magical, as if mixing Scarlet Crescent nail polish with Vermont lake water brought boys into your life.

"Hi," said DeWitt. "Your brother up to anything?"

"Why? Your summer going slowly?"

"It's always slow here," said DeWitt. "This is our thirty-eighth summer coming to this lake."

I looked at him long and hard. "Funny," I said. "I thought you were about my age."

"My grandparents own our house. Have for thirty-eight years. We have one big family reunion all summer long. The kids stay and the parents rotate in and out on weekends or during their vacations." DeWitt waved across the lake to the huge brown-shingled place with all the screened porches to combat the Vermont flies and mosquitoes. It reminded me painfully of Grandma and Grandpa's old house in Barrington. A

23

safe house. Where families had reunions, but never split up.

"It's an off month," said DeWitt. "Not one of my seventeen cousins is here. It's only me and the creep." He pointed to Veronica, who seemed rather proud to be labeled the creep.

An off month. What if we had an off reunion? What if they didn't make their own lemonade anymore, pressing lemon halves down on the old glass squeezer in the pantry, but just opened a box of powdered imitation lemonade instead?

"So it's just me and Veronica," said DeWitt. "I'm bored."

I nodded. In real life, a fourteen-year-old boy does not play with his seven-year-old sister. You have to be at a summer house to do that. And in real life, a fourteen-year-old boy does not hang out with a junior-high girl, either. All she can be is summer filler.

DeWitt was from New York, too, and we exchanged neighborhood and school information and DeWitt said he wouldn't be coming next summer because he'd have a terrific job instead.

I have never wanted to have a job. I don't mind when other people work, but I don't want to participate. I'll be fifteen next summer, but I have absolutely no plans.

I think life should be set up so you can choose where to stop. I am the only person I know who loved junior high, and I would have been willing to stay there indefinitely, being an eighth grader. Eighth is a relaxing year. You study only what you've studied before. I like that. I said this to DeWitt. He narrowed his eyes. Shortly after this he and Veronica paddled away.

DeWitt was the kind of person who would always be panting for the next stage, like Joanna. Angus is the kind of person who is so busy in the current life, he's forgotten past and future. And I like to sit and think, and watch things, and wonder, without actually participating all that much.

The sky was pale blue that day. Down on the dock where DeWitt left me there was not the slightest breeze, but high in the heavens a strong wind rushed the clouds along, as if they had an urgent commitment in another world.

I moseyed back into the house, where Angus was licking the icing from a cake Annette had baked. There's something about summer houses that entices you into the kitchen. Last night we had been up for hours making corn-tassel dolls because I had read about them in a Lois Lenski book. Maybe Vermont hours are slower than New York hours, or perhaps Vermont kitchens are more welcoming.

Angus ran his finger around the cake rim and scooped up a whole fingertip for me. I retrieved it with the tip of my tongue. It was yummy. Ever-so-slightly orange-flavored. "You know what Joanna said to me on the phone the other night, Angus?" I said. I took a finger scoop myself. The cake was beginning to look quite odd, with sled tracks where our fingers had plowed away the snow icing, and the chocolate earth showed through.

"What?" Angus got the milk out of the refrigerator. Vermont has excellent milk.

"She said she's always wondered if Daddy has a son by his first marriage, and she would meet the son one day and have a crush on her own brother." I poured us each a glass of milk. "Isn't that silly, Angus? The whole idea of Daddy having another kid?"

Angus gave me a very funny look. "But Shelley," he said, "Daddy does. His name is Toby."

Chapter 3

*V*ermont lay quietly around us, full of hot sun, shining lake, and the sound of Annette down by the water turning pages in her book.

I didn't want her in on this. I hissed, "What are you talking about, Angus?"

"Toby," he said. He began gathering supplies for one of his endless projects. He brought from the screened porch a beach chair. The low, folding kind where you sit with your bottom practically touching the sand.

"Who is he?" I whispered. "Toby who? What are you talking about?"

"I don't know. I just know he is."

"Is what?" I was shrieking now, but still whispering. Annette was aware of nothing. For that matter, Angus was aware of nothing. He rounded up two pairs of sunglasses, one to wear and one to perch in his hair. The pair he was wearing had miniature green venetian blinds so I had to look through the slots to see his eyes.

" 'But Shelley, Daddy does. His name is Toby,' " I repeated. "What kind of sentence is that? What do you mean?"

Angus pawed through the carton of broken crayons, dry Magic Markers, tracing paper, and construction paper. He extracted a relatively clean notebook and some pencils.

I grabbed his shoulder to get his attention. "Exactly how did you learn about Toby and what are the gory details?"

Angus shrugged as if it hardly mattered. "Dunno."

"What do you mean you don't know? Our father—the father of Joanna, Shelley, and Angus Wollcott—has a son named Toby as well and you don't know how you know?"

Angus nodded. He checked his pencils for sharpness.

If he didn't give me a real answer in a moment, I would check for sharpness by using them as weapons. "Angus, that is a lie. Information as important as that would stick with you. Especially with you. I bet you have a whole separate disk in your word processor for Family Secrets."

Angus looked thoughtful. He's always ready to take on a new project. But he shrugged a second time. "I have to get downtown," he informed me. "I can't waste any more time on this." He gathered his necessities, hanging the beach chair over his shoulder like a huge purple-and-green-striped handbag.

I tightened my grip on his arm but Angus threw me off. Last year he was a scrawny, thin, weak eleven-year-old. This year he's just as thin, but he can pin me to the wall, or the floor, or I suppose the lake bottom should he choose. I'm against it. Little brothers should stay little.

"But nobody can have a son and not mention

him!" I cried. "How about Christmas presents? And birthdays? And there's money—you have to pay for new shoes and braces for crooked teeth and band instruments. And wouldn't Grandma and Grandpa have noticed and said something? And Mother, during the divorce—our divorce—wouldn't Mother have mentioned that? She mentioned everything else on earth. She would have thrown in a son named Toby. I think you're making it up, Angus, and I think it's mean and cruel and horrible and I want to know the truth."

Angus hates to repeat himself. He always wants a conversation to be brand-new. "So ask Dad. He'll be home Friday night. I'll get Annette out of the way and you ask him," he said irritably. Angus was truly not interested. He was interested in the stars in the Vermont sky, and the fish in Vermont lakes, and the money in little Vermont pockets, but he was not interested in the incredible thing he had just said to me. *But Shelley, Daddy does. His name is Toby.*

Angus ran upstairs and I could tell he was rooting around in Daddy and Annette's room. He came down with a pair of binoculars.

It was the sort of collection that makes an older sister nervous, because who knew what Angus's latest project might be, and where he was planning to put that beach chair. Experience told me not to ask and definitely not to go along.

Angus's incredible sentences echoed in my head, banging around as if they were alone in there. As if I had no other thoughts, possessed no other knowledge.

I tried to see into his eyes to find truth and facts, but the sunglasses kept his secrets.

I resent sunglasses when other people wear them. They could be laughing at you, or ignoring you, and

29

you will never know. A black lid or a silver reflection instead of eyes. It's robotic. When people wearing sunglasses talk to you, you just want to rip them off.

But if *you* wear them, you live in another world, where you are the only one. Safe in the dark. You should always be able to wear your sunglasses, but other people should never be allowed to wear theirs.

I tried to think of a threat that would force him to talk but Annette came in. Angus stood in front of the cake so Annette wouldn't see the ski trails of our fingers. "I'm going to walk into the village for new library books," she told us. We nodded. Annette hesitated, hoping one of us would want to go with her, I suppose, or say something nice, but I was frozen by the specter of Toby, and Angus was too busy with his own plans. Annette left the house, pausing at the clump of orange tiger lilies where the yard turned into woods. We had tried putting them in bouquets, but they didn't last.

I thought she would never be out of sight. I turned to Angus but he was gone, out the other way, marching off by himself. He never cares what he looks like and he never cares if anybody goes with him. I like a friend along. In fact, if I don't have a friend along, I probably won't go.

I cut myself a piece of cake. It tasted just like cake. I drank my milk. It tasted just like milk.

I walked outside. The hedges were woven with honeysuckle and bees. The perfume and the humming crossed in the soft, quiet air. Waves made by a passing motorboat lapped over smooth stones.

I lay on my back in the high grass. I planned my conversation with Daddy when he came on Friday. "So, Dad. How was work? Written any good letters to Toby lately?"

30

It sounded so easy when I rehearsed it. A joke to which Daddy would give me the punch line.

But it wouldn't be easy to say.

Because what if it was true?

Or would I never tell, and pretend I hadn't heard, and it couldn't be?

I wasn't lonely, out there in the grass. How can you be lonely when the sun is shining down on you? But I was alone. The most alone I have ever been.

Angus's sentence made me afraid. *"But Shelley, Daddy does. His name is Toby."*

Fear is as isolating as sunglasses. I felt separated from the thoughts and eyes of the world. But fear isn't safe like sunglasses. It brings dark, but a dark full of menace. A dark in which your father is not what you thought.

I tried to think of safe things. If my friends from New York, Marley or Kimmie or Bev, were here, what would we talk about? Clothes, of course. What to pack for a reunion halfway across the nation with a family of Perfects. Safari jackets or elegant blouses? Torn blue jeans or sundresses?

The day crept on, slow and hot.

I tried to think of The Perfects, about whom we half joke because they are so flawless, and half envy, because it sounds so nice. I tried to think of August barbecues, and cornfields, and I reminded myself that Brett would be sixteen and probably have interesting friends who might think I was cute. I told myself Grandma always had great presents for the grandchildren and Aunt Maggie always had breathtaking amounts of food, as if she thought you couldn't buy anything fresh in New York.

Toby was under all my thoughts, like water under

a boat. You can look at the sky or the oars or your knees, but in a boat the water is always there, deep and cold and unknown.

In a way, because I could not share my thoughts with my friends or my sister, it was all less. And yet at the same time it was more, because it could not be diluted by hashing over the details a hundred times on the phone.

The sun faded, not behind clouds that would scud away, but pale and formless as a sheet hung out to dry. My world felt completely emptied, as if Angus had punctured it.

I telephoned Joanna without caring if I woke her up or not. That six-hour time difference can be really annoying.

She didn't mind. She told me about the latest fabulous restaurant in Paris and the newest fashions and the really terrific Impressionist paintings they had seen. "We went to Giverny," she said. "I walked through Monet's garden. I saw the very lily pads he painted."

I not only wasn't impressed, I didn't even listen. "Joanna? Angus said there really is a brother and his name is Toby."

"I don't believe it," said Joanna. "It would be just like Angus either to make that up, or to have made it up in the distant past so that now it seems real to him."

"But Joanna, you guessed the same thing yourself only a few days ago. It must have been based on something. What did you hear?"

"I don't know," said Joanna uneasily. "I made it up, Shell. I'm sure I did."

"You go ask Mother if she knows anything about it."

But Joanna didn't want to start anything. Why bring up anything difficult?

"If Toby doesn't exist, he isn't difficult," I argued.

"If he does exist and Mother never heard of him and she gets mad at Daddy for never telling her, it will be difficult." Joanna said I was not to worry about it, it was silly rumor, anything started by Angus could never be anything but rumor. She changed the subject. She wanted to talk about boys. Joanna always has lots of admirers and dates. She and Daddy argued solidly the year she was fifteen because he wouldn't let her date until she was sixteen. To celebrate turning sixteen, she called up every boy she'd had to refuse before and assigned each one a night! Joanna and Angus are never shy.

I can't imagine asking a boy out.

I also can't imagine asking my own father if he actually has another boy of his own. One he somehow forgot to mention.

"So," said Joanna, "any boys on the scene?"

It amazed me that she could stop thinking about Toby like that. But then Joanna is never taken in by Angus, and I always am.

"Well, there's this kid named DeWitt," I told her. "He paddles around now and then."

Joanna thought I was in the throes of first love. She demanded a physical description. I had not really bothered to look at DeWitt. "He's—well, he's this—you know—I don't know! I think he has a tan."

"Oh, well," said Joanna, "I suppose you're going to be a late bloomer."

Me, Shelley, a quiet bud amid the splendor of the flowers. But the flowers fade, their petals wilt, and their stems droop—and then I come out, beautiful and shadowy in the setting sun—the Late Bloomer. And all the boys look up, startled, and move toward me in the evening.

33

I giggled and Joanna admitted that she was not blooming much herself in Paris, where there were tons of boys and men and they all whistled and smiled and ogled but they didn't speak and she still didn't know them. I felt much better about Paris. Joanna would never stay long where the boys didn't ask her out.

I told her about my thoughts being less because I had no one to share them with, and yet more because they weren't diluted.

"Like concentrated orange juice," agreed Joanna.

"Like what?"

"Thinking about things all by yourself is like being jammed into the frozen orange juice can. But if you had friends to talk it over with, then it would be the whole gallon. You could pour off glasses and glasses without even noticing. It's more important when you keep things to yourself."

I begged Joanna to come to the Reunion and she said no and I said, "Well at least tell me what to wear," so she told me and I disagreed with every selection, which made me feel much better, and in control again, and I told her she had no taste in clothes and she said *she* was buying *her* clothes in *Paris* and that *equaled* taste, and we wrapped up the phone call with a nice screaming fight just like old times and I went back out in the yard feeling good again.

Annette and Angus came home together and they were both crying. I had never seen Annette actually break down and Angus probably hasn't cried since he was six. The dust from the road had risen around their faces and caked in their tear tracks. They looked like relatives now, by blood and not marriage.

"How dare you spy on me like that?" sobbed Annette. "You are so horrible, Angus."

"I wasn't spying on you," Angus wept. "I really wasn't. I was taking notes and making lists. I had a list of feet. How many people had shoes with laces and how many had shoes without laces and how many were barefoot. Then I had another list of how many people in Vermont are overweight compared to regular and of course I always carry my license-plate list with me. Like there's a dentist with a cabin on the lake and his plate reads GUM DZZZZ and you never know when you might find another like that and—"

"You were not!" screamed Annette. "You were spying on me. I came out of the psychiatrist's office and you had your binoculars trained on me."

"It was coincidence," whispered Angus. "It really was. Don't tell Daddy."

Luckily we still had some of New York City's finest chocolate chip cookies left from Daddy's last delicatessen trip, and I whipped out a plateful and glasses of milk all around. One of my grandmother's sayings is that all problems are more easily faced with a chocolate chip cookie in your hand. I said delicately, "A shrink's office, Annette?"

She whirled on me. "You think it's going to be easy for me to face all those people in Barrington? They all think your father's—well—his—"

"First two wives," I supplied.

"Were so terrific," said Annette, "and I'll have to show up with you two, and Angus will probably take his leg and—"

"They won't hold *you* responsible for my leg," cried Angus. "They'll say it's another sign of an unstable life and they won't blame you at all."

"They'll say *I'm* another sign of your unstable life," said Annette, reaching for a tissue.

We all dipped into the Kleenex box with her and snuffled and mopped up. I took a second chocolate chip cookie and Annette said weren't there any onion bagels left? and Angus said no, and anyway we were out of cream cheese. Annette actually checked the garbage for the discarded Zabar's bag that had held the onion bagels and I said Boston was only three hours away; they probably had a decent deli in Boston, and Annette said let's go.

So we all got in the car and drove to Boston to find a delicatessen.

"You know," said Angus six hours later, "you're not bad, Annette."

"I know my delis," said Annette. "There are those like you, Angus, who can scent a profit out there waiting—"

Angus's chest expanded, like a smaller version of Daddy's.

"—and those like you, Shelley, for whom cute teenage boys row around the lake—"

For whom *what*?

"—but I myself am a delicatessen finder of the very first order." Annette drew a blue ribbon on a paper napkin and draped it on her shoulder.

"Then I think Dad was wise to marry you," said Angus, "because that is a valuable skill."

Chapter 4

Angus opened a roadside stand to sell the scarlet and orange zinnias he cut from the back garden. For hours he sat holding an umbrella over himself to keep off the sun, surrounded by orange juice cans, soup cans, jelly jars, and ketchup bottles stuffed with flowers.

When cars didn't stop at the rate Angus wanted, he changed tactics, threw his umbrella down, and rushed out into the road, arms waving frantically.

Of course they braked now. This adorable, red-headed, freckled son of America probably needed either an ambulance or adoption.

The people in the first car (New York plates) thought Angus's zinnias were a free welcome-to-Vermont gift and they drove away without paying, exclaiming how sweet it was up here in the country.

The couple in the second car (New York plates) thought fifty cents was a lot to ask for half-wilted zinnias and drove away, exclaiming what a shame it was that even here in Vermont, children were obsessed with the Almighty Dollar.

Annette spent the day staring at a scrap of fabric she thought was very Country, blue and yellow, trying to decide if she liked it enough to do the whole kitchen in it.

I spent the day being jealous of Angus for having the kind of personality that could think up things like bomb shares and cockroach training pits and hidden half brothers named Toby. I was mad at myself for not asking Daddy the truth and mad at Daddy for not telling me to start with and wondering why I couldn't have a family like DeWitt's with seventeen cousins.

"Angus!" yelled Annette. "It's getting late. Come in and let's plan supper." To me she said, "He'll want to light a fire again tonight, but he puts so much lighter fluid on the briquettes that the flames go higher than the roof. I can't stand it again. We'll have spaghetti and tomato sauce instead of hamburgers on the grill."

If we lived in Barrington, I thought, we'd be going over to Aunt Maggie's all the time. Uncle Todd would already have the barbecue lit and the coals would be gray when we got there. We would be the ones to bring the salad and the dessert, and they would put on the steaks and we would be a big happy family all the time.

Grandma would come back to Barrington at least for the summer. Everybody would laugh a lot and play board games like Monopoly (which we can't play because we all get so determined to win we turn into animals and Annette quits).

Angus stomped into the kitchen. "How can I get rich selling zinnias?" he shouted. "Dad ruined all the real chances of earning real money. I hate Vermont." He kicked the table leg and slammed the door. "I don't want spaghetti, Annette!" he yelled when he saw her putting water on to boil. "I want tuna fish, peanut butter, and marshmallow sandwiches."

"That's disgusting," said Annette.

"You're disgusting," said Angus.

I wondered if The Perfects ever had conversations like this. I got the spaghetti out of the pantry. Italian food is so much more comforting than other foods. Your potatoes, now, they're not nearly as comforting as your macaroni. But the slurp of spaghetti trailing into your mouth and the little flecks of tomato sauce zinging across the table if you are Angus, who is a high-speed slurper, are very comforting.

Angus yelled at Annette for marrying Daddy. Annette yelled at him for *never* cooperating, *never* trying, *never* being a human person like normal twelve-year-old boys.

I put large handfuls of stiff spaghetti into the boiling water, poking it down with a wooden spoon.

Angus said he wanted peanut butter, marshmallow, and tuna, and that was the dinner he was having. He yanked the peanut butter off the shelf and began slathering it an inch thick on bread.

"How about a knuckle sandwich?" I said to Angus, forgetting how strong he had gotten. I slugged him and he slugged me back and then I was afraid for my life. I screamed for Annette to protect me, but of course she didn't feel this was her responsibility, so I had to put the table between myself and Angus for safety. Angus tried to flip the table and crush me with it.

"Stop it!" yelled Annette.

We didn't stop.

"At least don't fall into the boiling water," said Annette.

The telephone rang.

I thought it was Daddy, phoning from Canada, where he had gone on business. We each wanted to get our version of the fight in first and we all made a dive for the phone. Annette slipped in the Kool-Aid powder Angus had spilled earlier when he was trying a combination Kool-Aid and zinnia stand. Angus, vaulting over the table, put his palm right down into the sandwich half-spread with peanut butter and wasted valuable phone-answering time licking his hand.

So I got the phone.

But it was not Daddy.

"Granger Elliott here," said a man's deep voice. "Annette Fletcher, please."

Annette's maiden name was Fletcher. Granger Elliott was her boss before she quit to marry Daddy. He was at the wedding; he knew her name was Wollcott now. I glared at the phone and the Marine-sergeant way he had asked for her and handed the receiver to Annette.

Granger Elliott had such a booming voice that Annette held the phone out over the kitchen counter instead of up against her ear and we all heard Granger moan about how nobody was as competent as she was, nobody understood the job as well, and her replacement (third in as many months) was quitting. Could Annette please, please, please come back to him? She could name her price; he needed her.

Angus righted the table.

I stirred the spaghetti.

Angus stuck uncooked spaghetti through his hair, turning himself spiky and martian.

At the office, I thought, nobody will demand a tuna fish, peanut butter, and marshmallow sandwich.

40

Nobody will sell bomb shares. Nobody will row her out in the middle of the lake and then dive out and swim to shore, abandoning Annette (who can't row, hates the water, and feels the lake is out to get her) just as a thunderstorm is boiling up.

My hand was bruised from where I had belted Angus.

Brett and Carolyn probably never beat on each other. Never threw their dirty socks at each other, even. For all I knew, Brett and Carolyn never got their socks dirty to start with.

Angus opened a jar of Ragu tomato sauce with meat flavor. It popped when he broke the seal and he licked the inside of the cap. Angus prefers his spaghetti sauce cold. I put Parmesan cheese on the table and stuck the strainer in the sink. I decided we should have potato chips, too, and rummaged around for a bag of the ones I like, which are plain old-fashioned, as opposed to the ones Angus likes, which are ruffled.

Of course Annette will go back to work, I thought. We'll have one mother in France and a stepmother at the office. I'll be home with Angus after school, fighting over television and snacks. And next summer we won't come back to Vermont, because she won't have the vacation time. She and Daddy will go off alone for their two weeks, and we'll be shipped to Barrington, where everybody will know we're visiting because nobody else has time for us.

I ripped open the potato-chip bag so savagely that it burst like an angry volcano and spewed potato chips all over the kitchen.

Annette turned her back on the potato chips, and Angus, and me. "Mr. Elliott," she said, "I'm willing to discuss it. I can drive down to the city tonight, stay in

41

our apartment there, talk details with you in the morning, and still get back here to Vermont by suppertime tomorrow, for the children."

She's not too eager, is she? I thought.

I poured the spaghetti into the strainer.

Annette cast a long glance around the kitchen and it was an even bet she was looking for her car keys, not spaghetti.

"I'll call the Frankels next door," she said to us. "They won't mind if you spend the night. Where are your sleeping bags?"

Angus never hears anything he doesn't want to hear. "Oh, good," he said, "we're going to New York. I've always wanted to eat spaghetti in the car. I'll sort of drink it, so there won't be sauce everywhere, Annette. Let's see. I'm going to bring back my baseball-card collection. I can trade it for stuff, and then—"

"You're staying here," said Annette. "Make a list. I'll bring what you need."

"You can't leave us here!" said Angus.

Annette paid no attention. She was already on the phone to the Frankels, who obviously were going along with the plan. "Thanks so much," said Annette. "They'll be over as soon as they've had supper and cleaned up the kitchen." She paused. There were Frankel noises. "Great," said Annette. "Fine. Thanks a million." She hung up.

Angus threw his sandwich crust down on the table. Nothing much happens to bread crusts when you throw them; if he didn't get his way soon, Angus would throw something that made more of a statement, like Annette's favorite sugar bowl. "I haven't been home in a whole month," cried Angus, "and—"

"And you're not going now. I have things to think

about. I don't need the two of you bickering in the back seat, demanding to stop at every McDonald's and changing the radio station every ten miles."

Angus threw his zinnia money on the table. It spattered over the room. One quarter spun madly in the center of the floor. "I hate you!" he screamed. "You're always pushing us around. I wish I lived in France with Mother. You won't even let us go to New York with you, and it's our house, not yours. When I grow up, I'll never come near you! I hate you!"

Angus turned and ran out of the house. The screened door slammed so hard it bounced two times. Angus's feet pounded for a moment and then the sound was swallowed up in the deep grass.

Annette put her hands over her eyes and took a deep breath.

I wanted to go to New York too. I wanted to get together with Bev and Marley and Kimmie and tell them everything and—

"I don't have much cash," said Annette wearily.

We had to scrabble through everything. I gave her my seven dollars and we robbed Angus of thirty-six (Angus always has money; it's very mysterious) and I promised to say it was my idea so Angus wouldn't hate her even more.

"Eat your supper now," she said. "Maybe you should have a vegetable."

"Annette, will you just go?"

"Where do you think Angus is?" she said.

"Behind a bush, waiting for you to leave so he can have his spaghetti."

"Don't have a food fight."

"We won't have a food fight."

Annette seemed to feel she had settled all unpleas-

43

ant possibilities now. I know it never crossed her mind that I might think it was unpleasant for her to go back to work. We had always told her we would never miss her.

She drove off into the night.

The house was very dark.

The refrigerator hummed. The hot-water heater clicked.

Outside the lake lapped and the wind blew. The insect chorus screamed hoarsely. The woods swayed.

There was nothing between me and the night except flimsy screens on open windows.

"Angus!" I called *"Angus!"*

He didn't answer. He was good and mad, staying away for so long. Usually Angus was too hungry to vanish for more than half an hour.

I was afraid to close the windows and afraid to turn my back on the door. I couldn't lock it because Angus had to get back in. I wrapped the plaid football blanket around myself for protection and turned on the TV for company. Lying on the couch with my spine pressed into the pillows, I tried not to think about the black gaping holes of the house, where darkness sat looking at me.

"Shelley! Shelley!"

Mrs. Frankel was shaking my shoulder. "Shelley, it's after eleven o'clock. How long have you been asleep here? There isn't a light on in the entire house. *Where is Angus?"*

Chapter 5

We could not find Angus anywhere.

"Let's not get frantic," Mrs. Frankel said over and over. "He's got to be right here. Let's stay very, very calm." She skittered around the rooms of our house and hers, bumping into lights like a moth. She had been wearing a huge T-shirt for pajamas, over which she now had her beach robe. Finally she pulled on jeans and slid her bare feet into sneakers without taking time to lace them. She looked peculiar, but also comforting, the way people do when they have forgotten appearances and conventions. I hung onto my plaid football blanket and Mrs. Frankel.

Mr. Frankel drove the quarter mile into the village, as if Angus might be sitting on the curb in front of the drugstore at this hour of the night. We could hear his voice, worrying the night. "Angus! Angus!"

Nobody answered.

There was something terrible about the soft warmth

45

of the night, as if it were all a facade, and behind the blackness of leaf and stone, evil crouched.

When he got back home without finding Angus, Mr. Frankel put new batteries into his flashlight. He walked along the lakefront, casting the beam of the torch over the water, as if he expected to see Angus's torn sneakers sticking up in the silent wetness. He went down the dock, poking the light into the rowboat, and he went down his dock and two other docks, looking inside their boats.

Neighbors emerged from the next house over to help. "Angus?" they said, nodding, as if they had been expecting this sooner or later. "Has he run away?" they asked. "You call the police yet?"

My brother would never run away. It was not his style.

Mrs. Frankel said, "How much did he want to go to New York with Annette? Maybe he hid in her back seat."

"Or he's hitchhiking," said Mr. Frankel.

You should be pleased when police arrive within seconds of being called, but it made me even more frightened. There were so many of them, and they seemed so very anxious. A little boy gone after midnight had brought not only the police on duty, but roused others from their beds, as if their thoughts were the very worst.

But the police, when they heard about our family, were relieved. After all, they said to each other, these two kids were abandoned here—by a stepmother—left to the care of neighbors we hardly knew—father was not even in the country—off in Canada somewhere!

"Broken family," said the police, nodding to each other. "New Yorkers."

46

I flushed beet-red in the darkness of the yard. I felt responsible for the moral character of all New York City.

They'll never let us forget this, I thought. Because we're already not a stable family, and this is just more proof.

Mrs. Frankel could not figure out from all the phone numbers scribbled on our kitchen phone notepad which was for Daddy in Montreal. I didn't want Daddy to know. I didn't want Annette to know. It was my fault; I should have run out after Angus and coaxed him home.

"We've got to reach somebody," said Mr. Frankel. "Do you have any relatives we can call?"

"No!" I cried. "You can't call them!"

It would sound so much more awful than it was, especially if the police told it. *Twelve-year-old boy, red hair, ninety pounds, ran away from home. Father out of the country, mother lives abroad, stepmother en route to New York City. Supervision by fourteen-year-old sister who fell asleep.*

When The Perfects find out, I thought, they'll know for sure Angus and I are At Risk.

I could see Aunt Maggie and Uncle Todd as if I had a photograph album in front of me. Aunt Maggie would look lovely, even if they woke her up at this hour. She always contrived to look tailored, as if she had her own Parisian dressmaker, and yet very domestic, as if moments ago she had finished making her own fudge.

They'll blame Annette, I thought. Even Joanna and Mother and Jean-Paul will blame Annette.

I pictured Annette driving down the New York Thruway, one car among countless trucks, speeding toward the city, all unknowing, dreaming of going back to work, where she would be safe from the pranks and cruelty of her stepchildren. Now she'll *really* go back to work, I thought.

The untouched spaghetti was congealed and pasty-white. The jar of sauce lay on its side, telling all the world we were the unstable sort of people who ate out of cans, and whose parents didn't leave phone numbers.

Mrs. Frankel defrosted two boxes of doughnuts she had in her freezer, and made coffee, so everybody searching for Angus came and went with a doughnut in one hand and coffee in the other.

They searched in terrifying places. The trunk of the Frankels' car. The town dump. The scary trash alley behind the little grocery, close to the stream that is black and oily by night.

Around one in the morning, Mrs. Frankel finally found the right hotel in Montreal and told Daddy. Daddy said he would drive straight down and be with us in two hours.

I had forgotten that Canada is closer than Manhattan. My entire family was floating; I was the only one in place. Everybody related to me was drifting by night, location unknown.

I was so scared for Angus I could hardly breathe. Mrs. Frankel kept saying, "Now, now," but she was more scared than I was; when she held me for comfort, I could feel her heart beating faster, like a drum getting out of control.

The police got funny tight mouths, and squinting eyes, as if they could see better than I some of the terrible, evil things that could have happened to my little brother.

Oh, Angus, I thought. Did you try to sell time-shares to somebody with out-of-state plates, who'd had too much to drink? What forest did you run through? What deep water did you tumble into?

At two in the morning three DeWitts drove up. Grandfather DeWitt, Papa DeWitt, and our DeWitt. They were nothing alike; the grandfather was tall and trim, the father short and stocky, and my DeWitt just plain looked wonderful. "You okay, Shelley?" he said.

Nobody had worried about me. Angus was using up all the worrying energy. "Kind of," I said. I almost started to cry when DeWitt touched me. It was just the tips of his fingers on my shoulder, but my heart filled with weeping instead of comfort.

I couldn't break down! It would be unstable. I couldn't give the police or The Perfects or the Frankels any more evidence.

My DeWitt said, "I know this is dumb, Shelley. I know this must have been the first place you looked . . . but—you did check the bomb shelter, didn't you?"

Not one of us had remembered the bomb shelter.

"He's probably having chicken noodle soup right now," said DeWitt.

Three police, five neighbors, two Frankels, and I raided the bomb shelter.

Angus was wrapped in a green army blanket, sound asleep.

The rest of the night, we partied.

The police were too wired-up to go home to sleep. Mr. Frankel said events as emotionally draining as this called for Chinese food, and Mrs. Frankel said luckily she had a freezerful. Angus staggered around clutching his army blanket and refusing to be lectured for giving community-wide heart attacks. "You should have known I would go to my bomb shelter," he said reproachfully.

"We should have," agreed one of the policemen. "My daughter is one of the ones who wouldn't take her five dollars back. Although now that I see the salesman, I'm not sure it was survival she was interested in."

Everybody laughed hysterically and nuked some more Chinese food.

Angus shuddered dramatically at the idea that a *girl* could be of any interest to *him*.

DeWitt put his arm around me. "I'm the hero," he said. "I've always wanted to be the hero."

You can spend four weeks puttering around with somebody and not actually see him. DeWitt became a person for me. Thin cheeks and a sharp, aggressive chin, happy brown eyes beneath very heavy brows and shaggy hair, with a grin that spread the thin cheeks until they fit his forehead properly. His hand was very large, as if his arms still had a lot of growing to do to match, and when it rested around my shoulder it was a true weight.

He smelled of coconut from his suntan oil; a rich tropical scent that was completely out of sync with the Chinese food.

Mrs. Frankel refused to feed anybody who had said bad things about New Yorkers, so all the policemen apologized profusely; the two older DeWitts told Early Twentieth-Century Lakeside Living stories; my DeWitt enlarged upon the joys of Being A Hero; and Angus mentioned that all the Campbell's soup in the world was not useful without a can opener.

Which is why, when Daddy drove in, tires screaming, leaping out of his rented Canadian car shouting, "Shelley! Shelley! Have you found him yet?" there was

50

nobody home. We were all over at the Frankels' nuking ourselves some more Chinese food.

Daddy was a complete basket case by the time he finally found us. He kept hugging Angus fiercely, which embarrassed Angus, who did not want to be slobbered over in front of policemen in uniform. Then Daddy hugged me, and even lifted me off the floor, as if I were even younger than Angus. "Kept your head, didn't you, sweetie?" he murmured. "I'm proud. Stop shivering. It's okay now. Angus was just being a twelve-year-old."

There was no Chinese food left for Daddy. Mrs. Frankel said she could always get the chicken noodle soup out of the bomb shelter. DeWitt said maybe tomorrow he and I could go to a movie. Just to relax. Shrug off all this lakeside tension.

"I've thought up a good money-making business for you," Daddy told Angus.

Angus brightened. "Hey, great. What?"

"I've lost ten pounds in the last few hours. You could promise your customers to bring so much stress into their lives that they'll lose ten pounds overnight."

Everybody was sure Angus would be successful at that.

Chapter 6

"*W*hat is this?" said the airplane stewardess, although anybody could see it was a leg.

"It's my brother's leg," I said.

The leg was long, curvy, and slim, with red-painted toenails.

"Your brother's leg," she repeated. Tilting backward and squinting, the way grown-ups who need bifocals do when they read the newspaper, she peered down the leg from as far off as she could manage. She seemed to think there might be dynamite beyond the bend at the knee.

"I'm just holding it for him," I said.

Annette pretended to be having purse problems. She dropped back in line, shuffling through traveler's checks and credit-card receipts from things she bought last Christmas, and pencils without tips. She has one of those bottomless-pit handbags, almost a suitcase, that holds her entire life and part of ours. It matches nothing, so that no matter what Annette wears and how good she looks, the outfit falls apart the minute she hoists that handbag.

Angus raced up, waving the poster he had just bought in the air terminal gift shop. "I can keep it from getting wrinkled by stuffing it down the leg," he said happily. The stewardess watched silently while Angus slid the rolled poster into the leg. "Are you two going as unaccompanied minors?" she asked.

I saw Annette praying. "Sure," I said.

The stewardess saw her chance to be rid of us before the flight even began. "Then you have to have filled-out forms. Only the designated adults can pick you up at your destination."

Annette surrendered to fate. "They're not unaccompanied," she said sadly. "I'm with them."

Annette was wearing a white cotton dress of the Indian sort—a million gathers of thin, prewrinkled gauze. It was already limp. Her pretty necklace had twisted so that the clasp and not the pendant hung down the front. Her hair, pulled back in a narrow white scarf, had slipped out and was collecting in her face.

Nobody would believe she could control Angus. The stewardess patted Annette's shoulders and said she'd bring lots of snacks during the flight. Angus says that's why he behaves like this. Air hostesses are like zookeepers; they throw food at the little animals to quiet them down.

Angus is a great fan of food, especially airline food. He likes opening little packages and he cruises up and down the aisles asking people if he can have their salted nuts.

Annette and I have gotten extremely good at pretending we are not related to him.

53

This time, however, our seats were in the center row and nobody had a window or even an aisle. It was difficult to figure out what to do with the leg, as all packages had to be put beneath our feet or up in the luggage compartments for takeoff, and the leg didn't bend at the knee.

Angus made an effort to jam it into the luggage space above him. A businessman seated on the aisle between Angus and freedom stared with slack jaw at Angus standing tippy-toe on the seat, shoving at plaster toes.

It didn't work. Angus sat back down with his leg.

"I shouldn't have brought it," he said.

I stared at him. Since when had Angus cared whether or not he obeyed Federal Aviation Administration rules?

Angus quivered slightly. "They're going to laugh at me," he said. "The Perfects are going to think I'm a jerk. And I shouldn't have brought my collections, either. Don't tell anybody I have them, okay? Promise? We'll just pretend I didn't pack them." He turned a pleading face to me, his freckles blending in with his sunburn, and his summer-bleached eyebrows blond beneath the red hair.

The businessman opened *The Wall Street Journal* and folded it narrowly. It flapped momentarily in Angus's face. Angus didn't even see.

Angus had filled an entire suitcase with his collections, planning to show them to Brett. I could not imagine the sixteen-year-old boy who would care about a twelve-year-old's hoards, especially the peculiar things Angus considered treasure. I was relieved that we were going to keep it a secret.

Annette thought we should just abandon the entire suitcase at baggage claim.

"Let's not go that far, Annette," said Angus.

"Well, I'm mad at you," she said. "A rain dance is bad enough, but falling through the roof and now your father isn't coming till next week and I have to do this alone—it's too much, Angus."

By now the businessman had stopped pretending to read financial reports and was concentrating openly on our conversation.

"You're not alone, Annette," protested Angus. "I'm with you."

Even the businessman could see this was not a comfort to Annette.

Angus had videotaped an American Indian rain dance that was on public television. After watching it seventy-five times in a row, he had it memorized. Carrying his ghetto blaster for rhythm and noise, Angus went up onto the boathouse roof and danced, appealing to the gods of Vermont for water to combat a drought we were not having in the first place. The gods of Vermont must have found this irritating, because during a particularly frenzied period of stomping, Angus went through the roof.

He was yelling that he had broken his leg, and Annette and Daddy and the Frankels came running to the rescue.

I was extremely jealous, as all my life I have wanted a cast so I could be on crutches and hobble weakly and have my school books carried and be an object of attention and get funny signatures all up and down my plaster.

The only consolation was that it was still summer. With any luck Angus would have the cast off before school started and would thus gain no benefit from having gone through the boathouse roof.

However, once Daddy and Mrs. Frankel (on ladders) and Annette and I (inside the boathouse) pushed him all the way through (like Winnie the Pooh being shoved through Rabbit's hole by Christopher Robin), it turned out all he needed was a Band-Aid.

"It rained, though," said Angus proudly.

"It was already raining!" hollered my soaking-wet father.

Angus felt this was a mere detail, hardly worthy of notice.

What with one thing and another (fixing the roof, retrieving the ghetto blaster from the lake, comforting Annette that this was not her fault any more than Angus vanishing into the bomb shelter had been her fault), Daddy missed another two days of work. Added to the days he missed when recuperating from his midnight drive from Montreal, he had missed enough days that he said he would now have to miss the start of the family reunion. We would go on alone and he would catch up later.

Annette didn't yell at Daddy for abandoning her to the clutches of his unknown family, and she didn't yell at Angus for causing all this and she didn't yell at me for standing around doing nothing. She just sagged.

I could not bear it if she got all saggy when we met The Perfects. She had turned out so decent for a few weeks. I wanted to put her on display, like a new model car; let them drive her around a little, admire the paint job, try out the accessories, and agree that Daddy had done all right for himself after all.

The days before we left were strange and tippy.

Annette was preoccupied with Granger Elliott's job

offer. You could actually see her weigh the pros and cons as she tilted from one side to the other, studying an invisible balance sheet in the palm of her hand.

Daddy was equally preoccupied by the job offer. He said several times he had not married Annette in order to acquire an at-home mother for his children; he had married her because he loved her. But later on he also said he understood that she might want to go back to work, he knew it wasn't her fault that we had the lost boy/bomb shelter/Frankel night, nor my fault, nor Angus's—but if this was what happened just over an interview, what might go wrong once she was really working?

I called Marley and Bev and Kimmie, separately, and I meant to tell them all about Annette and her maybe working; and Toby, and his maybe brotherness.

But instead I listened to them.

Marley had a maybe boyfriend.

Bev had a maybe job as a model.

Kimmie had a definite boyfriend.

It's terrible to be the listener. It's terrible to have all you need to say stuck in your throat. You can hear, but not share.

They were my best friends, but something (Geography? Miles and mountains between us? Or loyalty? Privacy?) kept me from talking.

Grandma called from Arizona to say she too was on her way to Barrington and would see us soon. She assured Angus she had wonderful presents for us, and also a new video camera and a suitcase of film so that the entire reunion could be immortalized.

I know only little kids think about their presents instead of their reunions. I know I should have thought first of Grandma, and the joy of seeing her again, but her suitcase always yielded up the very best of gifts and I could not stop wondering what there might be this time.

Aunt Maggie called for plane-arrival details and said she had made so much potato salad we were going to drown in it, and also lime Jell-O with carrots, and shortcake for strawberries and homemade peach ice cream. Angus was so courteous he didn't even tell her he would die before touching lime Jell-O with carrots. He requested an entire gallon of peach ice cream saved just for him, and Aunt Maggie promised.

The reunion started to feel possible, and even fun.

I started remembering Barrington again, and planning things to do with my cousin Carolyn, and secrets to tell her—and got stranded constantly, like a swimmer at low tide, thinking of the secret that might or might not exist.

DeWitt said, "I can't believe you, Shelley! Why don't you just ask your father and then you'll know?"

"Sssshhhhh," I whispered. "Sounds carry over water, DeWitt. Stop yelling."

"Your problem is you don't yell enough, Shelley Wollcott," said DeWitt. He yanked in the oars and rested them on the bottom of the boat. Now that his hands were free, he put them on my knees instead. I was wearing baggy shorts in gaudy blue, yellow, and orange, and a huge white T-shirt that said Levi's 501. I was smeared with neon-colored suntan lotion because out on the lake I get burned, and I had on sunglasses because otherwise I have to squint so hard I get a headache. I didn't feel like me at all, but somebody else entirely, in disguise.

DeWitt's hands on my kneecaps tightened, and he

shook me, the way you shake people by the shoulders. It made the whole boat rock and we giggled. "I can't ask," I told DeWitt. "What if it's true? What if he really has another son? Because DeWitt, if it's true, Daddy *abandoned* that son!"

DeWitt felt knowing the facts would make it possible to deal with them. I didn't want to deal with facts. The facts of my life were hard enough without adding more to them. "Anyway," I said, "if it's true, then my father is bad."

DeWitt said it did seem to him, speaking of course just as an outsider, that my father had made more than his share of major errors, but—

"He has not!" I shouted. I jumped up to get rid of DeWitt's hands on my knees and DeWitt jumped up to yank me back, and New Yorkers that we are, we forgot about being in a tippy little rowboat and we flipped.

It is an effective way to get somebody's hands off your knees. We sank in the icy cold water and came up sputtering and casting blame on each other at the top of our lungs. Then we had to right the boat, which was a pain, and get our bodies back in, which was the most embarrassing exhibition of bad coordination in Vermont that summer, and bail it out and rescue the oars . . .

"I guess that's what it is to be unstable," said DeWitt, grinning. Lake water ran off his hair, got caught in his thick, wide eyebrows, and became little brooks going down the sides of his cheeks. He looked different with his hair plastered down. Older, and more interesting.

"I am not unstable," I said stiffly. I took the oars myself to ensure we would row back to my dock and not to his.

59

DeWitt leaned back dramatically, locking his hands to make himself a pillow. He stared up at the sky as if he were a young intellectual at an English university, being punted down the river. "I'm leaving," he said. "My grandfather is taking me and two of my cousins camping on the Appalachian Trail. And by the time you get back to Vermont from your family reunion, we'll have gone home to New York."

We had reached my dock. I handed him the oars and swung myself off. *"Gone home?"* I would never see DeWitt again?

DeWitt stood up in the rowboat, grinning so broadly his mouth was nearly as wide as his forehead. "You're going to miss me!" he shouted, singsong, the same melody as "I've Got A Secret." He rowed off backward so he could see me as he vanished. Loud as an opera star, he sang, "She's going to miss me, she's going to miss me!"

Several people on other boats and docks applauded.

Oh, he was as embarrassing in public as Angus. It just had taken him longer to show his true colors. I stomped off the dock into the house and let the screen door slam.

Joanna called very late that night. "Guess what?" she cried. I could hear her excitement all the way across the Atlantic Ocean. "What?" I said. It was startling to hear her voice. It wasn't the hour; it was that I had forgotten Joanna. In one short month, Annette, Angus, and I (with Daddy on weekends) had become a family. Joanna wasn't part of it. When she left, Annette had still been an interloper.

Interloper, I thought. Somebody who lopes around, getting between you.

"I'm coming too!" cried Joanna. "Isn't that wonderful? Aren't you thrilled? You guys were having so much fun over there, and I got jealous, and I'm tired of Jean-Paul and Europe and I don't care if I go to the theater in London or anywhere else, so I'm flying Paris to New York to Chicago to Des Moines! I'll get there only forty-eight hours after you do! Isn't that great?"

The phone sat in my hand. Terrible thoughts flew toward my tongue and I choked, keeping them silent.

I don't want Joanna to come now. I want to be special. I'm never special. Joanna's the oldest and Angus is the craziest and I'm just Shelley. If Joanna comes she'll be friends with Carolyn and run around with Brett and find out about Toby and stay up late with the grown-ups sharing memories.

I swallowed. "That's great, Jo."

I wanted it to be great. I wanted to want my older sister around. But I didn't anymore.

What an awful age fourteen is. Everybody changing shape, like summer becoming fall. My shape was changing without my permission; I did not even know whose daughter, whose sister, whose girlfriend I was. I never asked for different parents or different schools or summers separated from my sister. And now, equally without my permission, without even my noticing, the posture of my love for Joanna had changed too. I did not want her next to me, in charge of me, older than me. Am I growing up? I thought, dimly, against tears, or getting mean?

"I know," said Jo smugly. "I'll take a limousine from the airport to Barrington."

"A limousine?"

"Well, actually it's the airport long-distance bus, but they call it a limo. Mother bought me a wonderful new wardrobe. All the latest Paris summer styles. Wait'll you see my sunglasses, you'll die. And my shoes. This way I can be the oldest, Shell, and we'll push Annette into the corner and let her fade there. We'll show those Perfects a thing or two."

She's going to be Perfect also, I thought. In her Paris clothes, after her European vacation. She'll be part of them, not us. "Annette's not so bad," I said to my sister. Would we have gone to Boston for bagels if Joanna had been home? I wondered. Would Joanna have let Angus carry his leg around or get locked in the bomb shelter?

This is why we didn't get along with Annette. Joanna wouldn't let us. "Tell me about the sunglasses," I said to her.

There won't be any time for me now, I thought. Whenever there's time, people will ask Joanna about Paris and the Eiffel Tower and chateaux on the Loire.

And I knew then that nobody would squeeze lemons for lemonade either; they would dump imitation lemonade powder into the Tupperware jug and swish it around and toss it over the ice cubes and it wouldn't count.

It was a strange flight.

Angus didn't notice his salted peanuts, let alone beg for more from the entire plane. Annette got out her cross-stitch; she is forever making authentic Early American samplers to frame in dark wood and put on the walls. During the entire flight, she never got around to threading the needle.

I wondered if Daddy really did have business he couldn't miss for these three or four days. Or was Daddy scared of his own family reunion?

I thought about DeWitt, who was even now trudging in the heavy boots he was so proud of over the rocky crests of Vermont hills.

If only I had discussed DeWitt with some other girl: my sister or my friends in New York. The memory of his company would be more real if I'd told Kimmie or Bev about his hands on my knees, and flipping the boat, and bellowing "She's going to miss me!" But I had kept it to myself and now it hardly counted at all. It, and DeWitt, were truly gone.

Over DeWitt, who never touched any part of my body except one shoulder and both knees, I got a lump in my throat.

I had bought *Seventeen* for the plane trip and never opened it. Joanna would have the glamour cornered. *Oh Grandma, I'm too big to sit in your lap now and anyway you sold the wicker rocker when you moved to Arizona.*

The plane landed.

It was so bumpy the whole plane held its breath and exhaled in unison once we were definitely down. My hands had gone cold.

Angus said, "I think I'll just slide the leg under the seat and abandon it."

Annette and I were not about to argue with that.

Angus tilted the leg until it went sideways on the floor between two seats. It looked horrible; a piece of body, as if detectives would find the torso and arms later.

At least The Perfects were not going to witness us with the leg. We shuffled down the skinny red-carpeted aisle, following the arm of the airline terminal. I hate those portable hallways. They're like monsters, sucking you up into luggage control. "Is my hair all right?" whispered Annette.

Her hair looked terrible. "You look great, Annette," I told her.

She got out her purse mirror to check. "I look awful. You're being kind. You know you've really touched bottom when a stepchild is kind."

"There they are!" shouted Angus, running ahead, darting between luggage trolleys and flight attendants. The Perfects were in a row, just as I had pictured them.

Grandma was as plump as ever, hair whiter, her arms held out for Angus. Aunt Maggie was brunette and beautiful in a sleek white linen dress with navy accessories and fragile sandals. Uncle Todd was in khaki pants, safari shirt, and sneakers so white he must have bought them an hour ago. Carolyn, laughing, her hair more golden than I remembered it, looked cool and only partially interested. Perfect people probably never went wild the way Angus was right now.

I was determined to be Perfect also. I would make Annette be Perfect. I would kill anybody who said a single syllable about Daddy being anything other than Perfect. I put on my calmest smile and advanced smoothly, as if I were on wheels. This would set the pace for the whole visit.

The Perfects swooped upon Angus, shouting and hugging, while Annette and I held back.

I'm afraid, I thought. Why am I afraid?

Because it's like school. It's a test. *We're* Perfect, are *you?* What's *your* score?

"Shelley, Shelley," said my grandmother, her voice choked and joyful. "Oh, Shelley, honey, I am so glad to see you. You look so lovely!"

My eyes misted over. It was going to be all right. Grandma had not changed. We had never needed to

64

be Perfect for her. I was shocked to find myself taller than Grandma. She would not be holding me—I would be holding her.

But it was the reunion I wanted most, reunion of the most perfect kind. "Oh, Grandma," I whispered.

"Wait!" cried the stewardess, racing up to me, grabbing my sleeve. "You forgot your leg!" she cried, thrusting a long, pale, curvy thigh into my arms.

Chapter 7

*U*ncle Todd and Angus were in the garage workshop drilling, because Uncle Todd said the leg would be easier to carry around if it had a rope sling. "Oh, you mean like a submachine gun," said Angus happily, "just casually thrown over my shoulder."

Grandma was napping. She said she napped every afternoon now, and the long drive to the airport and all the excitement of seeing us again had really tired her out.

Brett was no place. He hadn't met us at the airport and he hadn't been waiting at the house, either. Nobody commented on this.

Personally I think they just didn't want to be close by when Aunt Maggie finally exploded. She had managed to stay calm and even pleasant all during the explanation that no, Daddy wasn't with us, and no, he would not be coming for several days, and no, we had not realized she had a huge Surprise Party planned just for him—tomorrow night when he would not be here—we had thought the only party was her Twentieth-Anniversary Celebration next week.

Annette, Carolyn, Aunt Maggie, and I sat primly out back, sipping iced tea, which I happen to loathe. The tall frosted glasses were pretty, though, with slashed lemon circles adorning the rims.

The backyard was nothing like I remembered. Gone was the torn and sagging badminton net. Now there was a large in-ground pool, with blue tiles and yellow stripes underwater. We sat beneath a yellow awning, gazing at the towering oaks and a single fluffy cloud in the vivid blue sky. The poolside furniture was sleek and modern. The house itself was air-conditioned now, so the hummy whir of window fans was just another memory, soft and vibrating in my past. "But where are the swings?" I said. "And the hammock and the old tire and the sandbox?"

Carolyn and Aunt Maggie laughed. "We got rid of those years ago," said my aunt. "Children of divorce, I notice," she informed Annette, "always yearn for the safer, more controlled parts of their childhoods."

Annette squeezed a little acid from her lemon into her drink.

"It's just like Charlie to do this to me," Aunt Maggie said, looking unhappily around the yard. "A wonderful surprise party planned for tomorrow night because you people said you were going to be here, and now Charlie won't be! All his old high school friends invited—and no Charlie!" Aunt Maggie looked surprisingly like Joanna. She pouted in just the same way, lips puffed out on the bottom and tucked in at the top. "I should have known Charlie would vanish just when I need him. Charlie is never there when you count on him."

I stopped being polite about the nasty cold tea and poured it into the grass. "Daddy is always around when *we* count on him," I said.

"Shelley, you don't have to defend him to me. I understand your father extremely well." Aunt Maggie told us forlornly about the special touches she had arranged just for the brother who was too cruel even to come.

"I suppose that's the basic problem with surprise parties, isn't it?" said Annette. "The main character doesn't always fall in line with the plans."

"But you told me you'd be here!" she repeated. "I have forty guests who are driving or flying in just to see Charlie."

Forty guests with joke gifts and expectations—and I would have to make excuses for my father.

Annette and I said nothing. What defense was there?

If Aunt Maggie acts like Joanna as well as looks like Joanna, I thought, then I know what will happen next. She'll forget what she's mad about and get stranded inside her frown and stare about in a confused way. It was one of Joanna's nicest traits. Angus was always capitalizing on it.

Aunt Maggie stared about in a confused way. "Maybe we should all jump in the pool and cool off," she suggested. "Carolyn, tell Shelley about all your swimming awards this year."

Carolyn looked uncomfortable. "Mom, she's not interested in that."

Aunt Maggie said, "We're very proud of Carolyn. She's doing superbly."

Annette said she would like to hear about the swimming awards.

68

Carolyn said she would rather hear about Joanna. What had Joanna been doing all summer? Aunt Maggie said how wonderful that Joanna would be flying in in a few days. "It's so exciting!" cried my aunt, tossing her hair like a high school cheerleader waving a pompon. "Every few days or hours something special will be happening."

If you're a late bloomer like me, you think a lot about age, and whether people match their own age. I was an eighth-grade girl in a going-into-ninth-grade body. Aunt Maggie seemed like a middle-aged body with a ninth-grade girl inside it. Any moment she would talk about classes and boys and whether she ate the nutritious stuff in the school cafeteria or just had potato chips. Is that why she's on the school board? I thought. To stay a teenager?

"Shelley has had an interesting summer also," said Annette, sounding like a stage prompter.

"I've just poked around," I said. "But Angus sold time-shares in a bomb shelter and almost became a millionaire."

Aunt Maggie did not find the details amusing. "Surely this sort of sick prank could have been prevented," she said, frowning. "Is it wise, do you think, for Charlie to be away so much?"

Annette said she thought it was wise for him to earn a living.

Aunt Maggie said she was worried about how the children were turning out, scattered around the world before we were even out of our teens.

I could feel her getting ready to discuss our stability, or lack thereof. "Annette is thinking of going back to work," I said, to change the subject.

Aunt Maggie was appalled. Not only did we have to have a stepmother, the woman had hardly arrived before she was running off.

Carolyn jumped up, whether creating a diversion or totally losing interest I could not tell. "Well, I'm off to take Shelley to the pool, Mom," she said, "unless you have errands you want me to run before the party. Drive us there, okay?"

Aunt Maggie jiggled her glass to make the ice cubes dance. "We put in this beautiful pool," she told Annette, "but you know how contrary the young are. Still hanging out at the town pool just like before." She tried to laugh, but her heart wasn't in it.

Aunt Maggie forgot that Carolyn wanted a ride to the town pool and began telling Annette the details of a problem facing the school board. Whether to add another classroom to the crowded junior-high building, or (gasp! shock!) allow seventh and eighth graders to be *in the very same building* as the high school students.

"Oh," said Annette sweetly, "are the children here in Barrington all on drugs or something? You have to shelter the younger ones from the older? What a shame."

I decided Annette was going to be fine.

Carolyn and I went into the house to change into bathing suits. I was to sleep in Carolyn's room and Angus in Brett's and Annette alone in the guest room till Daddy got there. Grandma had the family room in the basement and the big bathroom down there. "Where is Brett, anyway?" I said.

"We'll see him tonight at a Little League game. He's a coach. What color is your swimsuit?"

The house was cool and dark. Full of possessions precious to cousins I hardly knew. Photographs on the wall of people I could not recognize.

Carolyn's room was extremely neat. Everything was folded, or rolled, or stacked. All colors matched.

"Do you like your stepmother?" she said.

I never use the word stepmother. I detest both halves of it. She's in no way my mother, and *step* sounds as if we're walking on her. "You mean Annette?" I said.

Carolyn giggled. "You have more stepmothers I don't know about? That sounds like my uncle Charlie."

All of a sudden I wanted to go home so bad I was afraid I would cry. My throat got hot and tight and my contact lenses scraped my eyes. I wiggled into my swimsuit and tugged the jeans back over it. I don't know these people, I thought. I don't want to know them, either. If I went into the backyard right now and said, "Come on, Annette, let's go," she'd be packed in a heartbeat. We'd throw Angus in the back of the rent-a-car and go to Disneyland instead.

Carolyn wanted to know if I knew how to ride a bike and I said yes, as a matter of fact her very own father had taught me how right in her very own driveway about ten years ago. "Didn't your own parents have time?" said Carolyn.

We cycled through Barrington, among lawns green from sprinklers, and hedges that grew too fast for clipping. Trees were so tall and leafy they made tunnels over the streets. In Vermont the trees fought for sky, but in Barrington each tree was far apart, taking all the space it wanted. Each was a separate work of art, not a mass of woods. Grass grew beneath Barrington trees, instead of the insatiable undergrowth of Vermont. Barrington seemed more civilized.

We passed burger and taco places I didn't remember and a gas station big enough to refuel the state of Vermont. We turned right at the elementary school, which had not changed. It had the shuttered look of unused schools over summer. Hot and dusty inside, books waiting, chalkboards clean, chairs stacked.

When I was little I used to daydream that we would live here and I would go to that very school.

I'm too old now, I thought. I never will go there.

At the pool, Carolyn bought us hot dogs and french fries from the concession. She slathered hers with ketchup and I whitened mine with salt and we joined her friends. I got that sick, tight feeling you have when strangers cast a bored eye on you.

Carolyn surprised me. "This," she said proudly, waving at me as if I were a fashion model coming down the runway, spotlights casting mysterious shadows on my high cheekbones, "is my cousin Shelley."

They said hello, and how was your flight, and how long are you staying? Then they went back to talking to one another.

Carolyn looked as if I had failed her; as if she had expected me to win friends and impress people from the moment we arrived. She and three others left to play tennis on the courts beyond the pool. I could see her through the high green vinyl wires and low shrubby roses that even in August had a few pink blooms fighting the midwestern sun.

"Now let me get you straight," said one of Carolyn's friends. She tapped her teeth with the earpiece of her sunglasses, which she used as a stage prop rather than as shades. "You're the cousin whose father—gosh, I've forgotten the details—what was it he did now? All kinds of things, huh?"

I remembered her name. Miranda. "Most people forty-five have managed to do all kinds of things, Miranda. You have to fill the years somehow."

Miranda smiled. She had small, pointy teeth, like a baby's. Good thing she didn't need braces; there wasn't space on the teeth to fit the bands. In an infantile way she was cute. Her hair was extremely thin and straight so that when she moved her head, which she did constantly, it was like shifting satin. Her eyes were bright and gloating. She knew something I didn't know.

I stared beyond the pool, and the tennis courts. The color of Barrington in August was not green except where sprinklers slowly whirled. The color of August here was sunburn—grass, hills, and fields toasted golden-brown. A field far off was the color of butter. Dust rose from the highway.

"Think I'll swim a little," I said. It was clear none of these girls actually swam. They decorated the pool rim, they tanned, and they wore bathing suits, but they didn't swim. "Coming, Miranda?" I knew she wouldn't come.

I made myself walk off slowly. I slipped into the water slowly and held my temper and my fear. Then I swam three laps, also slowly, because I am a weak swimmer, but maybe Miranda would think I was oblivious to her.

When I climbed out, Carolyn was still playing tennis. Her friends were still tanning. There was nobody to join. I sat on the pool edge.

Travel is such a strange thing. We had left Vermont before breakfast and arrived in Barrington before lunch. An entire life was not only hundreds of miles away, it also felt hundreds of years away. My

73

father seemed terribly distant, as if he really might be the person Aunt Maggie said he was, never there when you depended on him.

A bunch of high school boys charged out of the locker room like a football team crunching toward goalposts. They were Joanna's age, and all cute. Joanna would have adored them and it would have been mutual. I graded the selection for her. One definite ten, a nine, and the rest eights. Wow. Some high scores. Barrington definitely knew how to do boys.

I myself have never had a date.

I hear about Joanna's, of course, and I'm part of her plans and hopes and clothes and hairstyles, because we share a bedroom and she can't help it and neither can I. But dating never seems to apply to me. I look at boys but have never really felt like acquiring one of my own.

Last year in school we had to take Health, which is a graduation requirement. We skipped quickly over the tough Health subjects (like sex, AIDS, or pregnancy) and went straight to the easy Health subjects (like relationships). How I hated that class. I felt as if the Health teacher chose the entire curriculum to throw at me. "Children of divorce," she told us several times, "especially if it is the mother who has abandoned them, have a poor self-image. They fear affection. They shrink from love."

I wanted to scream, My mother did not abandon me! She abandoned Daddy. That's true. But the first two years, when she and Jean-Paul lived just two blocks away and we saw her all the time, that wasn't so bad. It was when Jean-Paul had to go back to Paris . . . even then she didn't abandon us; it was just that she couldn't have us and Jean-Paul too.

74

But of course I said nothing in class. In fact I got a bad grade there for Not Participating, when the truth is I remember everything she said better than Shakespeare, or the preamble to the constitution.

Sometimes when I am very sad, and the covers on my bed aren't heavy enough, or warm enough, or cozy enough, I think . . . *she did abandon us.*

Sitting by the swimming pool, abandoned by a cousin I didn't know to Barrington High kids I didn't know, I folded myself over and studied my toenails. I had painted them glossy rose-red and some of it was chipping off.

If Joanna were here, I thought, she'd be developing a crush on one of those adorable boys. She'd be laughing their way, flirting like mad. Is the Health teacher right? Do I shrink from love?

I flipped one toe in the water and watched the water bead on my skin.

One of the boys sat next to me.

The one I'd graded nine.

I was resting my chin on my drawn-up knees and I just barely turned to look at him, so now it was my cheek resting on my knees, my hair falling almost to the pool rim.

He was very tan, and all the hairs on his chest were sun-bleached gold. His nose and cheeks were slathered with zinc oxide and his sunglasses were pulled to the tip of his whitened nose so he could look into my eyes. He was like an adorable golden retriever, still wet from the pool.

For one of the first times in my life, I was aware of myself as a woman. A pretty one. Wearing my new parrot-colored suit. My tanned-in-Vermont skin turning pinky under the much-hotter Barrington sky; my hair frizzy from the humidity, so that damp corkscrews of light brown hair blew against his legs. I didn't shrink. I said, "Hi."

"Hi, there. You must be Carolyn's cousin." He had a deep voice, as if he needed to clear his throat.

I could not imagine how he could know that. Had Carolyn pointed me out from the tennis courts? Had Miranda said something mean? Or in Barrington did everybody literally know everybody, and I was the only stranger in town that morning?

"Yes," I said. I floundered around for something to say. "My brother's here too," I said desperately.

How ridiculous. Angus wasn't here at all; he was with Uncle Todd. And why did I have this need to put my little brother into a conversation? The Health teacher is right, I thought, I'm shrinking.

"Hey, great," said the boy. "I'm coming to the party tomorrow night. For your—um—dad. Looking forward to meeting you." He pushed his sunglasses back up and hid his eyes.

I sat up straight and drew my hands under my hair to flip it back over my shoulders, the way Joanna does. "I'm afraid he won't be there," I said. "Aunt Maggie planned the party without consulting us and my father isn't coming for several more days."

"Oh, no!" said the boy, but he was laughing. "That sounds like Mrs. Preffyn. I've tangled with her. So it's just you and your brother?"

"And my father's wife. Annette."

The sunglasses came down his nose again. His eyes were such a gleaming brown that they seemed to have tanned along with his skin; they were the same color as

August in Barrington—buttered toast. "Is that how you refer to her? Your father's wife?"

I nodded.

He nodded.

We could be a duet, I thought. I wouldn't mind. Ten days altogether we'll be in Barrington. Is that long enough for a summer romance?

I felt as if DeWitt had been sent to me as a training ground, like army basic. I had spent the requisite number of hours with a male person and now I could move on to the real battles.

He was—this boy—instantly a boy. I saw him completely as a person of the opposite sex who made me breathless and excited and happy and scared. Would it be that way from now on? Like Joanna, would I see each boy the way a grocery shopper sees peaches? This one isn't ripe, this one has a bruise. Here. I'll take this one! Would the world change now, like a nearsighted child looking through glasses for the first time—in one gesture passing from blur to sharp focus?

"You have stepbrothers or stepsisters?" he asked.

"No, thank goodness. It's hard enough having a stepparent without having to pretend there really is a Brady Bunch and we can all be joyful together. Besides, my real brother is enough of a pain." I told him about Angus: bomb shelter, leg, rain dance, and all.

"I wish I had a family like that!" he exclaimed, laughing. "But I'm the only child. Nothing ever happens in my family unless I make it. I don't have that kind of personality."

"Few do," I said. "For which we can all be grateful."

We laughed together.

I was supporting myself partly with one hand on

the wet tiles. He rested his hand there too, and one of his fingers overlapped mine. His hand was as hot as the burning sun and yet I shivered.

Maybe this is love at first sight, I thought. I can forgive everybody everything if this is what it leads to!

Carolyn came back.

She knelt down between us.

"Hi, Toby," she said. "Thanks for baby-sitting the cousin for me."

Chapter 8

The cousin.

Sometimes you hear men refer to their wives like that. *The* wife. I hate that.

What I needed to know was—was this *the* Toby?

Who knew the answer? Who wouldn't laugh or smirk when I asked? Who wouldn't give me a long list of all the things my father had done wrong? Who would give me the answer I wanted, which was that Angus had made up his Toby, and this Toby, another Toby entirely, sat beside me because he liked me, neither more nor less?

But Toby, whoever he was, vanished with his friends, and Carolyn and I pedaled home to change and help with dinner, although Aunt Maggie was so organized there was nothing to help with. Annette and I stood on the grass while Carolyn and Aunt Maggie fixed the picnic.

Joanna's prediction echoed in my head like a drumroll at a parade. "I always used to think that Daddy and Celeste had a son they never told us about. And somehow I would meet him, all unknowing . . ."

First Carolyn covered the large redwood table with a scarlet cotton cloth with weights sewn in the corners so it wouldn't blow away. Then she took four white runners, which she thumbtacked right across the table, making eight place mats altogether. Vertically down the center, making a plaid, she tacked a narrow brilliant blue ribbon. It was pretty and patriotic, but somehow very young—something a Brownie Scout might do, and not Carolyn, who was so careful to be sophisticated.

Why didn't I ask Daddy about Toby? I thought despairingly. I wished I could talk to DeWitt, out on the lake, me whispering and him shouting, the smell of barbecue drifting over the water. But DeWitt was gone.

It was very strange, but I believe at that moment, as Carolyn patted the picnic table, that the loss of DeWitt, whom I scarcely knew, was as dreadful and piercing as the loss of my mother.

"I thought of this color scheme," said Carolyn, as if she personally had invented red, white, and blue. "When I was in kindergarten. We've done every single picnic ever since just the same way. When I was little I used to color in the white paper napkins with my own designs but I don't anymore." She showed us lovely white cloth napkins on which a child's artwork had been embroidered. "Mother immortalized my masterpieces," said Carolyn, giggling at the lopsided, madly grinning stick figures.

My eyes got misty. We don't have any family traditions started when I was in kindergarten. After Mother left, nobody felt like keeping anything up, and Annette hasn't started any new ones. Besides, once you're as old as I am, it's too late.

Carolyn and Aunt Maggie went back into the kitchen for more trayloads. Annette fingered the embroidered napkins. "That is so sweet. When I have a baby, I'm going to do everything like that, too."

I practically fainted. "*When you have a baby?* Are you—I mean—you and Daddy—you're—"

"No," said Annette sharply, "and don't start any rumors. But I might. Someday. I love kids."

I thought this was very brave of her, considering what the three kids she knew best had subjected her to for the last year and a half.

It was all too much.

Too many people, too much coming and going, too many worries. I felt the way I had at age eleven, during the divorce, when both my parents were right and wrong, and we loved them and hated them too; when sleep was never restful and meals were never peaceful.

Angus raced into the yard brandishing a tennis racket. "Uncle Todd is teaching me how to play!" he shouted. "Uncle Todd says I'm a natural. Uncle Todd says I'm probably going to be a tennis star pretty soon." Angus swatted invisible tennis balls with great vigor.

The tennis balls felt real, bouncing off me, bruising me. My father gone, my aunt pouting, my cousin abandoning me, my stepmother sagging—Toby, a new baby, Joanna coming in Parisian clothes . . . I wanted to sob instead of think.

"Shelley, darling, are you all right?" said my grandmother. "It's the heat, isn't it, darling? Barrington is such a furnace in August. Civilized people can just hardly survive in backyards in August. Come sit in the shade with me, sweetie. You and I haven't had a chance to talk yet. You must tell me everything."

I made myself skinny so I could lie on the chaise longue next to Grandma, and even in the fierce heat it was so wonderful to snuggle and be soothed. Grandma said a person couldn't be too careful in all this sun and that I looked a little pink to her. She hoped I wasn't the kind of girl who got obsessive about a tan, because too much sun was very very bad. When was I coming to visit her in Arizona? She had missed me so much!

It was pretty nice to have somebody worrying about me besides me.

I stared at Grandma's hands. Her veins stood out, knotted blue against her age-spotted skin. Her knuckles were twisted and her rings swung loosely on her arthritis-curled fingers.

Grandma is old, I thought. I never knew that.

At the surprise party everybody would say to Angus and me, "My, how you've grown!" but they would say nothing to Grandma. You couldn't say, "My, how you've aged!"

I wanted myself always in eighth grade. I wanted Grandma always on her old front porch, laughing while our roller skates dented the floor.

No changes, I thought desperately, please no more changes. I can't go through any more changes.

"Now, after supper," said Uncle Todd, setting hamburgers on the grill, "we can't play tennis, Angus, because we'll be watching Brett's Little League team. He coaches Town and Country Gas."

"He what?" said Angus.

Carolyn gurgled with laughter. "The teams are named for the sponsors who provide uniforms and ice cream. We're very big on ice cream and T-shirts here. Win or lose, you get ice cream and a T-shirt. Tonight they're playing against Crest's Septic Service. Those guys have a motto printed in maroon letters on their T-shirts: SEPTIC PUMPING IS BEST WITH CREST."

Angus was reverent. Nobody else in New York would have a T-shirt that said that. He wanted a T-shirt like that too.

"It won't be an exciting game," warned Carolyn. She passed potato salad, and Angus, who hates mayonnaise, gagged. She passed deviled eggs, and Angus, who hates hard-boiled eggs, gagged again. "Better fix me six or eight hamburgers," he told Uncle Todd. "There's nothing else to eat."

"Why won't it be exciting?" asked Annette.

"Because they're only ten. If they even hit the ball, we stand up and cheer, but mostly they only get to base by being walked."

We were eating, and passing plates, and carefully not using our embroidered napkins, because they were too good actually to be used, when I realized Grandma was filming the whole thing. I started choking and she laughed and put away the video camera. "The minute you get self-conscious the film's no good," she said. "Anyway, I'm hungry." She sat down next to me, and it was difficult for her to swing her legs over the picnic table bench. Uncle Todd held out a hand to guard her against falling.

"I'll do the camera!" cried Angus eagerly, and he spent the rest of the meal with the camera on his shoulder, taking close-ups of people chewing. I had a feeling this would be a film Aunt Maggie would somehow never get developed.

"Time for presents!" announced Grandma. She gave me a little hug. "You have to have lots of good food first," she said to me, "so you're calm and happy for opening presents. Then you rip off the ribbons and the paper and see your new treasures and you top it off with cake and ice cream."

"My kind of schedule," said Angus.

Aunt Maggie took the camera, which amazed me, as she did not seem the type somehow, and filmed Angus opening his gifts.

He got four James Bond videos, which made him ecstatic, because Annette is sick of renting him James Bonds and now there won't be anything she can do about it if he wants to see them a hundred times in a row. He also got a pogo stick, which he immediately hopped himself into the pool on, and surfaced still bouncing away in the shallow end. And finally, a tennis racket and lots of balls.

"This is better than Christmas," said Angus, hanging up his pogo stick to dry and hugging Grandma fiercely, the way Daddy has taught us to hug. "Easy," said Grandma, holding up her hands. "I'm not as young as I used to be."

And I had thought the biggest change at the family reunion would be lemonade from powder. Some of Grandma had gone by, like the color of trees in autumn. She was closer to winter now.

"Gather round," said Grandma. "Shelley's gift is small." She handed me a velvet box, the size of my spread hand, and I opened a clasp that was shaped like a princess's crown. Inside lay a necklace of gold lace, with fragile tendrils of seed pearls dangling from it, and in the center a delicate row of larger pearls lying on a gold ribbon.

"That's a present?" said Angus scornfully.

"That's beautiful!" I cried. "Is it very old?"

"It was your grandfather's engagement gift to me, Shelley. But it isn't the kind of thing people need in retirement communities. I want you to have it. You'll be going to proms and this is the kind of necklace for very special nights like that."

"She has just the neck for it, too," said Aunt Maggie. "Long and fashion-model."

"You'd have to have the perfect dress," I said, holding up the filigree of the gold.

"Very, very, very low-cut," added Carolyn.

"Not that low-cut," said her mother, and we all laughed.

"This will be such fun," said Annette, touching the lacy gold curlicues. "We'll spend months shopping for the perfect dress, Shelley. Promise me not to find the right dress the first afternoon we go."

I promised. Carolyn got to hold the necklace, and then Aunt Maggie. I remembered my grandfather. "Grandma," I said, getting teary, "it's wonderful. Thank you so much."

"Don't cry, darling," she said, holding me and the necklace close. But I cried anyhow, and for a horrible moment I thought everything painful was going to well up in me, and I might cry for days or even weeks.

"Don't get mushy," said Angus. "Yuck."

"Girls do that," said Uncle Todd. "You get used to it. Come on, everybody, quick clean up, we've got to get to the game."

Grandma stayed home, because she was tired, but the rest of us got in the shiny new van and headed for the baseball diamond behind the elementary school. Green-painted bleachers held a few parents and some reluctant brothers and sisters. The sun was going down, the heat was tolerable, and there was a nice breeze. All the little players hit their bats against the ground to

85

make dust storms, and all the coaches squatted about giving advice nobody listened to.

"Which is Brett?" I said.

Carolyn pointed. "Blue and yellow. Baseball cap on backward. Come on, we'll sit with the other guys." From Aunt Maggie's canvas hold-all, Carolyn grabbed us two cans of soda and a pack of cupcakes.

I knew Annette did not want to be deserted so I didn't meet her eyes when I deserted her. We clambered over the bleachers to the top row on the far side, where a dozen giggling older kids sat in the shade of a huge oak. Behind me I heard Annette being introduced to somebody. "Oh, Charlie's new wife!" said a cooing woman. "How sweet."

Among the kids sat pointy-toothed Miranda. "Oh, the cousin," she cooed. "How sweet."

I wondered if Annette and I were now wearing the same fake smiles.

"So, Carolyn, a little family solidarity, huh?" said Miranda, smirking.

Carolyn sat on the bleacher in front of Miranda, presumably to avoid looking at her nasty little face.

"Brett get his car back yet?" said Miranda, leaning down, poking her pointy nose up next to Carolyn's.

"No," said Carolyn woodenly.

Miranda burst into a flutter of giggles, like pigeons when you go through them on the sidewalks. "Your cousin Brett," she said, turning her pointy nose into my face, "believes that anybody who obeys the rules of the road is just a coward. You should see Brett drive. Of course, you won't, because his father took away his car, and Brett moved out of the house and is living with Johnny Cameron, and of course the perfect

86

Preffyns aren't admitting that they have sort of a problem with their son—"

"Shut up, Miranda," said Carolyn.

Miranda was not the shutting-up sort. "Old Brett was chalking up points by hitting old ladies, Seeing Eye dogs, and toddlers in diapers," she said gladly to me.

"He was not!" hissed Carolyn. "He took the corner so fast his tires screeched and scared the old lady and when she tried to run she stumbled on the curb and that's how she broke her ankle. Brett did not hit her. Nobody hit her. And Brett called the ambulance. So there."

"*Now* you're saying that," said Miranda. "At the police station, you were first in line to lynch your own brother you were so mad at him for not being a Perfect Preffyn."

By now we had missed the first inning. I glanced at the scoreboard. It didn't matter. Nobody had gotten to first, let alone made a run. So we weren't the only ones to tease the Preffyns for their Perfection.

I could hardly wait to tell Annette about Brett. What ammunition! Not just a flaw, but a huge, gaping—

Midway between the parents and us, on a middle bleacher, sat my brother. Angus was slowly wrapping himself in toilet paper. He had used half a roll, and both legs looked as if he had plaster casts. He was working on his left arm. He finished the arm and began working on his forehead.

Carolyn was too busy defending her brother to see. I have defended a brother in my time. It's humiliating, and necessary, and you hate your brother for making you do it, and you'd hate yourself if you didn't.

"If you say anything more about Brett, I'm going

to sock you so hard you'll need dentures, Miranda. So there," said Carolyn.

Carolyn had pluses I had not suspected.

Angus now had a huge white bandage over most of his head. He bit open a tiny white packet and held it up to his forehead. Take-away ketchup from a hamburger place. Fake blood.

Miranda and the other kids noticed him. "Who is that?" whispered Miranda.

Carolyn and I said nothing.

Miranda thought we should locate the parents in case the little boy was insane.

My soda can was perspiring against my ankle. I picked it up, held it way down low, and began shaking it in the hidden space between me and my cousin.

Miranda said, "Ooooooh, look! Brett's team is going to make a homer!"

The homer was going to occur because nobody in the outfield could catch or throw. All the parents stood up and cheered madly for everybody and anybody.

"Miranda, you have a little brother or sister on one of these teams?" I asked her.

"No, I just like to come."

"She likes people around to pick on," said Carolyn bitterly. "Everybody has a skill; that's Miranda's."

"Thank you, Preffyn," said Miranda, smirking, her tiny teeth exposed like little beads.

From beneath the camouflage of my hair, I studied Miranda. She was watching Brett. In fact, she seemed fascinated by Brett. Having spent the last several hours myself thinking of nothing but Toby and DeWitt, I was pretty sure what was bringing Miranda to Little League games starring ten-year-olds.

I finished shaking my soda can.

Miranda said to Carolyn, "Has your mother actually admitted yet that Brett has moved out forever and doesn't even plan to return to finish high school in the fall? Has the chairman of the school board actually said out loud, 'Yes, my son is a high school dropout'?" Miranda's little smirk and pointy nose and beady teeth were directly between my face and Carolyn's.

I held up my soda can. "Want a sip, Miranda?" I said. I yanked off the pull tab.

Soda sprayed two feet in the air.

Miranda got so much soda her hair dripped. It soaked into her T-shirt and ran down her dangly earrings and hung like brown diamonds from her eyelashes. All the honeybees in Barrington deserted the trash cans and the flowers to get better acquainted with Miranda. She stood hopping ridiculously, waving away bees, crying, and threatening my life.

Carolyn didn't stop grinning for the rest of the game.

Chapter 9

*T*heir family room had the television, the VCR, the stereo and compact disc player, the computer, the synthesizer, and the fireplace. It was the sort of place where everybody sat separately with headphones or keyboard and did his own thing. Your old-fashioned people could start a fire and toast their toes or their marshmallows while your up-to-date people could run a few programs. Wedged among all these possessions were three enormous recliners, which, when tilted back with footrests up, missed the various components by inches. Once you were positioned in a recliner, you stayed there, fed by the person closest to the kitchen-door exit.

Uncle Todd's recliner was dark and leathery, and Aunt Maggie's recliner was flowery and ruffled. Carolyn and Annette and I fit together on a double recliner—sort of like an upholstered hospital-bed couch. Annette looked as nervous as somebody using a ski lift for the first time, and I was trying not to laugh because the tilted postures were so ridiculous.

That was before I tried it.

It was the most comfortable, cozy, wonderful way to sit. I felt deliciously decadent, like a Roman reclining for a feast. "All we need are the slaves," I said longingly.

"Angus," suggested Carolyn. "Is he well-trained?"

Annette and I laughed.

Angus, of course, was busy trying out headsets, and heard nothing as he tried to synthesize, compute, sort through the video selections, and start a fire all at one time.

Grandma said what with the air-conditioning being on and so forth perhaps we didn't really need quite as many logs as that on the fire, but Angus was safe inside his earphones and added every piece of kindling there was. Grandma sat in her straight-backed chair (she said she couldn't slump anymore, at her time of life) and watched Angus with love. "Aren't twelve-year-olds wonderful?" she said.

"I love twelve-year-olds," agreed Aunt Maggie. "I wish Brett were still—" She broke off.

Oh, good, I thought. We're going to talk about Brett, and solve all the Preffyn problems, and Annette and I will understand, because we've been through so much, and—

Aunt Maggie wanted to know what Carolyn would be wearing to the reunion party tomorrow night. "Not that it matters," she said gloomily, "since Charlie won't even be here."

"Let's tell Uncle Charlie stories," said Carolyn eagerly. "I bet Annette hasn't heard them all." She passed Annette a big wicker basket of that horrible homemade pretzel stuff you make using cold cereal and peanuts. Annette quickly passed it to me. I handed it on to Angus. He makes an excellent garbage bag for food nobody else wants. What fun this will be! I thought. At real family reunions, you always have to tell When Your Father Was A Boy stories.

"Uncle Charlie was the black sheep of the family," said Carolyn to me, happily.

Suddenly I lost interest in When Your Father Was A Boy stories.

Carolyn heaved herself out of the recliner, and crawled over her father's extended feet toward the kitchen, where she began hunting down more-acceptable snacks. "Everybody was always mad at Charlie and he was always having to run away or get divorced to escape."

Annette said she thought that was an oversimplification of the facts.

Uncle Todd said maybe he would tell some Carolyn stories, like the time when she sneaked into the state fair without buying a ticket on a day when the police were trying to corner a gang of teenage pickpockets and—

"Daddy!" said Carolyn, truly alarmed. "Stop it."

Uncle Todd said to me, "I think you can see your poor father has become a Barrington myth. And of course from what I see of Angus, there is some possibility of a second generation joining him."

"Was he that bad?" I said.

"He's terrific," said Uncle Todd. "Speaking of course as a bystander. Charlie's kind of like Angus. You're never bored. And of course people just don't know the facts of situations like Toby, because along with everything else Charlie keeps a great secret, and that means gossip." Uncle Todd pulled a lever on his recliner, moved slowly into upright position, and stood up. "Think it's time for bed now," he said. "Your grandmother looks a bit tired and we need to give her back her bedroom."

Angus was encased in his own noise and did not hear the word Toby. Carolyn and Aunt Maggie didn't look interested, and Annette was yawning. Grandma stood very slowly, looking longingly at the sofa, which would flip out into a bed for her. Uncle Todd shoved furniture around and popped Grandma's mattress out. Aunt Maggie straightened the sheets and pulled pillows out of a closet.

Ask! I ordered myself. Ask.

That's all. No big deal. Toddle along after Uncle Todd, who is definitely the Good Guy in this family, and say, But Uncle Todd, what exactly are the facts in the Toby situation? I know it's my father, but he kept his secret with me too. Is it a good secret or a bad secret?

The most crippling part of my personality is that as much as I want to know something, I can't bear admitting I'm ignorant. It's as if I think I should have been born knowing and understanding all. As if when I say out loud, what are you talking about? the world will point and jeer.

Uncle Todd thought Daddy was terrific and never boring. I totally agreed. But how could a hidden half brother be a good secret? How could it ever be anything but bad?

And yet there seemed to be nothing hidden about Toby at all. He was here and they knew him and Carolyn was friends with him.

Ask.

* * *

But I didn't.

We all drifted up to bed, except Angus, who wanted to stay up all night playing with machinery. Annette would have said yes, since it was vacation and who cared, but Aunt Maggie was the sort who believed that firm bedtimes made stable characters, so Annette said, "Angus! Certainly not! It's bedtime."

Angus looked as if he had not encountered this concept before.

"And you have to get clean first," I said quickly, expecting the horror of bathing to keep Angus from saying, "What do you mean, bedtime?"

Angus surprised us all by saying, "Oh, good! I get to use the bathroom first!"

Annette and I stared at him.

"They have a whirlpool," explained Angus. "You don't need a washcloth, even. It just flicks the dirt off you."

Aunt Maggie said you still needed a washcloth, and even soap, and if Angus needed any help, she—

"I don't need help!" yelled Angus, racing upstairs.

"What presents did Grandma give you?" I asked Carolyn.

"I want to take the train out to Arizona next time instead of fly," said Carolyn. "I want to look out the window. So I got train tickets. How come she didn't give you anything, Annette?"

"I'm kind of old for midsummer presents," said Annette. "Anyway, she's not my grandmother."

"She's your in-law," Angus said.

Carolyn giggled. "Grandma has had so many

94

daughters-in-law with Charlie she can't be giving presents to each new one every summer."

Annette said, "Thank you for sharing that, Carolyn."

The Preffyns do just what we do, I thought. We use them for our family joke. The Perfects. As in, "You wouldn't catch The Perfects having food fights, now would you?" They use my father for their family joke. As in, "How many wives is he up to now? Has anybody kept count?"

It seemed fine that we should laugh at them, but not fine at all that they should laugh at us.

Aunt Maggie came into the hall. She was wearing a lovely robe, satiny and lacy, like a bride, and holding high on a padded velvet hanger a summery dress with tiny tucks and flared skirt. "For tomorrow," she said. "You like it?"

We liked it.

She's going to have to laugh off Daddy not being here, I thought. And pretend that she's not upset about Brett. She'll be just like Joanna. Beautiful in perfect clothes, leaving a trail of perfume behind her, and nobody will know that she's cut into pieces inside.

"Great," I said gloomily. "I forgot my contact-lens holder."

Aunt Maggie frowned. "Didn't you make a list of what not to forget, Shelley?"

Nobody in my family can ever even find paper, let alone make lists.

We didn't bother to answer her.

Annette said, "There are two little water glasses in our bathroom. Put your left contact lens in the glass on the left side of the sink and your right contact lens in the glass on the right side of the sink and in the morning we'll go to the drugstore or something and buy a new case."

She may not be able to live with cockroaches or return bomb-shelter money, but she's good on the practicalities of life.

Carolyn and I climbed into our beds. We meant to talk all night, and Carolyn started by showing me her baton because she spent six weeks in baton-twirling classes before she saw a photograph of herself and decided she didn't want to be remembered in high school for her ability to catch sticks. "Like a dog," she said. "Brett kept introducing me as his sister the dog."

We started laughing, and then we started sleeping.

I have cried myself to sleep many times.

It was the first night I laughed myself to sleep.

It was much quicker. And much nicer.

It was cousinly.

Chapter 10

"Angus! Angus, come back here! You creep! You rat! You scumbucket! Come back here so I can kill you! Somebody stop Angus!" I threw my empty suitcase, hoping to maim him, but it missed.

The whole household poured out of bedrooms and breakfast room to see what was the matter. Aunt Maggie let Angus slip right by. People are always letting Angus slip right by.

"Stop him!" I screamed. "He drank my contact lenses!"

"Don't be silly," said my aunt. "Contact lenses are solid."

"Not when they're floating in water!" I said. I reached the back door. But I was blind now, and Angus nothing but a pale blob hurdling the shrubs and vanishing across the wide backyards of Barrington. "I hate you, Angus Charles Wollcott!" I shrieked.

"Shelley," said Aunt Maggie, "Shelley, please act your age. Fourteen-year-old young women do not—"

"They do when they're Angus's sister," I said. *"He drank my contact lenses."*

Aunt Maggie suggested we should all calm down, and have blueberry pancakes and a nice, leisurely Saturday breakfast.

"I can't see the blueberries," I hollered at her. "I could be eating marbles, or bird droppings. Anyway I want to get dressed and find Angus and beat him black-and-blue."

Uncle Todd wanted to know how this could have happened.

Annette said, "Shelley forgot her contact-lens case, so she used the two glasses in the guest bathroom."

"And Angus forgot on purpose," I said bitterly. "You don't know him the way I do. You can't tell me he was so thirsty he had to drink from both glasses. He knew he was drinking my contact lenses. Bad enough he had to become a toilet-paper mummy at the baseball game, but now this!"

Carolyn thought before we killed him, we should make him go to the bathroom all day long and I could sift through the results and get my contacts back.

Grandma said before we killed him, we had to catch him, which looked to be quite a task.

Uncle Todd said if he knew twelve-year-old boys, we could just set out food, same way you trapped any other animal.

Aunt Maggie said her philosophy of rearing children did not include violence and she did not want to hear any more of this unpleasantness.

"I reasoned with Angus last night," I pointed out, "and even with all that reason in his brain, Angus still drank my contact lenses."

Aunt Maggie wanted to know if we could telephone Daddy in Montreal and Annette said hastily that Daddy would be much happier if we handled the contact-lens crisis without him, and she, Annette, would take full responsibility for all eating and drinking of contact lenses in the family.

Aunt Maggie strong-armed us onto the chairs at the breakfast table. For a woman who does not believe in violence, she is very forceful. We had bacon, grapefruit halves, hot biscuits slathered with butter, panfried potatoes, blueberry pancakes, and tall glasses of orange juice. I don't usually have that much breakfast in a week. Grandma told about how my father used to hold lawn-mowing races with his best friends and once got so excited he mowed away the entire garden of the next-door neighbors. Aunt Maggie said that very garden owner was coming to the surprise party tonight with a little plaque commemorating the event, only of course Charlie being Charlie, he would not be present to receive it. Grandma told about the three times Daddy ran away from home when he was in high school. "Didn't usually go very far," said Grandma, smiling. "We found him one time sleeping in the garage."

I didn't think my father sounded like a bad and terribly scandalous person. I thought he sounded like a lot of fun.

"Squinting is not becoming, Shelley," said my aunt. "Stop trying to see without contact lenses and go get your emergency glasses."

I haven't worn those glasses for a year. Horrid misshapen yellowy rectangular atrocities that make me look like a mass murderer.

Annette said as soon as we were all dressed we would go into town and find an optician.

People began leaving the breakfast table. Grandma

went to her room and Uncle Todd said he had to change the oil in the car. They were blurs for me, their robes fluffy swirls, like watercolors on wet paper. Carolyn was the blue smudge near the refrigerator and Aunt Maggie the pinkish cloud over by the sink.

Next time I see Toby, I thought, I won't. He'll be a smudge like Carolyn. Great. I can be the first girl on earth to be in love with a golden blur.

Aunt Maggie burst into tears. I knew this by sound, not by sight.

"Now, Mom," said Carolyn uneasily. "Brett has to come home eventually. Just because he wouldn't even talk to us at the Little League game doesn't mean he'll never live at home again. Johnny's parents will get sick of feeding him, and Brett's grown another inch and needs new clothes and Johnny's parents surely won't buy somebody else's kid new jeans and sneakers. So Brett'll have to come home."

"He won't have to," said Aunt Maggie. "He could be just like his uncle Charlie, and wander around town wearing clothes that don't fit, and slicing open the tips of his sneakers so his toes poke through."

I giggled. "Did Daddy ever do that? He won't let Angus."

"Remind me to drag out the photograph albums," said Aunt Maggie. "I'll show you your father in all his teenage splendor." She sounded a bit grim. As if Daddy's idea of splendor when he was Brett's age had been pretty low-life.

Aunt Maggie burst out, "Brett thinks your father is somebody to *admire*! He thinks Charlie is something *special*! After all the hard work bringing my children up right, my own son turned out like *Charlie*!"

"I have been brought up right also," I said, but I said it very softly and Aunt Maggie didn't hear me.

"I have to give this stupid party!" she said, sniffling, putting dishes into the dishwasher as if she really wanted to smash them over somebody's head. "I had such fun planning it, and thinking about it, and getting all the details perfect—and every guest there is going to know my son doesn't want to live with me anymore and my brother couldn't be bothered to show up. Working weekends! Hah! You tell me your father really has important enough business that he can't show up here Saturday and Sunday!" She slammed the door of the dishwasher shut, jarring the glasses, and stormed out of the room.

There was a silence. By blob identification, I felt it was safe to talk; only Carolyn, Annette, and I were left. "We'll have to call her Big Joanna," I said. "Absolutely identical temper tantrums." Annette giggled. Carolyn wanted a detailed explanation, and my stepmother and I took turns telling her, and we all three laughed insanely, and then got dressed and went out to find an optician.

All morning we giggled about brothers, sisters, aunts, and uncles. We found contact lenses. It always seems odd to me that glasses take days to special order, but contacts you can take off the shelf. We spotted Angus buying a Dairy Queen but decided not to kill him after all. Carolyn waved at friends of hers, and Annette offered to let her out, but Carolyn said no, she had set aside her friends for the week I was visiting.

Set aside her friends.

Joanna and I had not done that when Carolyn and Brett visited us in New York. We had never even considered doing it.

101

A cousin is a very special thing. A girl who hardly knows you, and yet she matters more, and is more, than some of your friends.

Last night after the Little League game, when Brett stood all dusty among his losing players, and his parents walked uncertainly toward him, I saw in his face what Annette must have seen in mine and Joanna's and Angus's for a year and a half. Sneering rejection. Oh, how I understood Brett! You have so little power when you're a kid; you can't hold together your own mother and father's marriage, or prevent their marriage to strangers, or keep them from dividing the china and the property—but you can curl your lip, and see them wilt, and see them hurt, and it's good.

It's strong and it wins and you're glad.

But this time I hurt for Carolyn the peacemaker, caught in the middle. I hurt for Uncle Todd, who was being nice to Angus. I hurt only a little bit for Aunt Maggie, though, because she was doing exactly what Joanna had predicted she would do: saying bad things about Daddy.

Carolyn gave Annette driving directions, and pointed out important landmarks, like Miranda's house, and Johnny Cameron's, where Brett was living.

"Where's Toby's house?" I said casually.

"Oh, he lives in Chicago. He's just visiting. You knew that. Don't tell me you didn't know that," said Carolyn.

Annette turned left and headed back to the Preffyns'. "Who's Toby?" she said.

Carolyn gave her a funny look. "Well, you know," she said vaguely, "Toby." Then she gave me a funny look, as if Carolyn and I knew something my stepmother didn't.

Carolyn knows. They all know. That's why Daddy isn't here. He's chicken. The son came to meet him, and Daddy is afraid.

The moment we walked in the door, Aunt Maggie told me to call Paris.

Call Paris! I thought. What does that mean? Call my mother? Call Joanna? Hasn't she left yet? Is her plane stuck in Iceland or Atlanta or something? Is Mother ill?

My head whirled.

Driving around Barrington, I had started to think of Annette as my stepmother.

Maybe it's not such a bad word after all, I thought. A mother, but a step below. I don't want her to go back to work! I want her to stay with Angus and me, and be in Vermont, and forget Granger Elliott, and take us bagel hunting in Boston.

Have a baby. Could she and Daddy really do that? Well, of course they *could*—after all, I had had that year of Health; I knew they *could*—but ... my father, who was the most wonderful father in the world ... could he really have had a son Toby whom he ignored for the next eighteen years?

No, no, no, no, not Daddy! I thought, and I dialed Paris and prayed that I would not have to talk to Mother because I had enough adults in my head, too many adults in my head; I—

Joanna answered.

I heaved a sigh of relief.

But her sigh was even greater. "Oh, Shell, I'm so glad to hear your voice; I feel as if I've been here a century. And Shelley, I can't come home. I'm not going to join you in Barrington."

"Can't come home?" I whispered. *Not at all? Not ever?*

"Mother started crying when I said I wanted to be in Barrington more than I wanted to be with her, and she hasn't stopped crying and—oh, Shelley, it's so awful, I hate it when parents have feelings. I think they should be like carvings. Solid. No emotions." Joanna swallowed. "So I won't be getting back till we planned. September the eighth."

I remembered that now I could keep on getting all the attention.

"Mother needs me," said Joanna desperately, as if she was afraid I would never speak to her again without a better explanation than that.

"Oh," I said.

Joanna said Mother was crushed because of my attitude.

"Mine?" I said. "I don't even have an attitude."

"Yes you do. You're maddest of all of us."

"I am not. I don't even care."

"You do too. You think I've shared a bedroom with you without hearing you cry at night?"

"Why didn't you say something? I would have cried quieter. It's none of your business if I cry, Joanna Wollcott!"

"See, you're mad," said Joanna with satisfaction. "You're basically always mad, Shelley."

"I am not!"

"Uh-huh. Tell me. When we finish talking, are you going to ask to speak to Mother?"

I was silent.

"Because you're mad," Joanna informed me.

But I was not mad. Mad is hot, and trembly, and violent.

I was only lonely. I wanted Joanna to come after all, and my father to come right now, this minute. I wanted explanations. Annette not to go to work. Toby not to be my brother.

"So I'll be in London after all," said Joanna drearily. "Mother says her three children have gone and grown up without her and she doesn't know us anymore, and we'd all prefer to be elsewhere."

"What did she think would happen when she crossed the ocean without us?" I said. I thought of all the things Mother didn't know. Like Angus turning from a thin little boy to a sturdy future tennis star. "I'll miss you, Jo."

"Bye," she whispered.

Our voices matched. Hearts on diets.

"Say hello to Mother," I told her.

Chapter 11

I went into the kitchen. Everybody was there but Angus—Grandma, Uncle Todd, Carolyn, Aunt Maggie, and Annette.

"Is everything all right?" said Grandma anxiously. "Joanna isn't ill, is she? Or your mother?"

I shook my head. If only people would tell you their feelings without you having to ask them! If only Grandma would tell me what she thought about my mother, about Paris, about the divorce. I wanted so much to hear.

But I could not bear asking. My biggest flaw. I just couldn't put the sentence together, tag on a question mark, lift my voice, and demand answers. I couldn't do it in school, I couldn't do it with my father, and I couldn't do it here either. "Joanna's not coming, that's all," I said. "She's going to go on to London with Mother and Jean-Paul, that's all."

"That's all?" cried Grandma. "Oh, Shelley, but that's

terrible! We've been looking forward to seeing Joanna so much!"

"And hearing about Paris and all the exciting things she's done," added Aunt Maggie.

"And trying on her clothes," said Carolyn wistfully.

They all talked about what a loss it was not to have Joanna coming. They talked about the loss of my father and the loss of Brett. Of holes in families and pain and absence and distance.

I could not bear it. *I'm here!* I wanted to shout.

I went out of the kitchen, through the back porch, and into the backyard. What had made Brett run away? So his father yelled at him about bad driving and wouldn't let him use the car after all. Did you leave home and school for good just because of that?

I, who had just told Joanna I never felt mad—I had outgrown being mad—I was mad enough for the whole town of Barrington.

And maddest of all at Daddy.

You should be here! I yelled at him in my heart. You're making Annette and me defend you! You're ruining the party. You're not telling me who Toby is!

Carolyn came out with me. "Listen to my parents in there talking about Brett again," said Carolyn, waving toward the kitchen. "It's driving me crazy. How come they can't talk about *me*? *I'm* the one doing things *right*."

I could not keep my muscles still. I wanted to strangle something, or beat it up, or cream it.

I had a sudden memory of my mother, years ago, making pound cake. She had beaten the butter and sugar together with a wooden spoon and never used the mixer. "Does it taste better that way?" I had asked, licking the bowl. I was probably seven or eight at the time; I know my feet didn't reach the floor from the stool. "No," said my mother. "I just feel better. Pound cake is a cake for when you want to pound somebody, and instead you pound the batter in the bowl."

Oh, Mommy! I thought.

I wanted to be back in time, to be seven again, while my mother wore the old red-and-white-striped apron with the bib, and beat the bowl, and gave me the spoon to lick.

I turned my head away so Carolyn wouldn't see me cry. "Let's go for a walk," I said.

Carolyn stared at me. "I suppose we could," she said doubtfully, as if she had walked once a few years ago and maybe the skill would come back to her. People who live in cities walk much more than people who live in towns, even towns like Barrington where everything is so close and there are lots of sidewalks.

"We'll be back later, Mom," Carolyn shouted back at the house, but nobody heard, and we just wandered away. Carolyn looked up and down the yards and intersections as if she were a tourist.

"I haven't done this in ages," she confided.

We walked block after block. On the far side of the road, surrounded by thick evergreens and a vast stretch of lawn, was a stone church with slate sidewalks and a glass-fronted announcement board for Sunday services. "Our church," said Carolyn. "Do you go to church? We get to skip summers but during the school year we have to go to Sunday school."

We had never been to church. I was uneasy about admitting this to a Preffyn; no doubt churches were like backyards, a necessity for stability that Daddy had omitted.

"You know the parable of the prodigal son?" said Carolyn.

I didn't even know the words parable and prodigal.

Carolyn shrugged irritably as if she had known I would turn out supremely ignorant. "It's two sons. The bad one leaves home; he parties, takes drugs, hangs out with scums. The good one stays home and does all these chores for his father. One day the bad kid comes back and says he's sorry and the father is so happy he throws a big party. But all the time the good kid was being good, the father never even thought of throwing a party for him."

It didn't sound like a religious story to me, but then I knew very few.

"I bet anything," said Carolyn fiercely, "that I'll stay home being good forever and the most they'll ever give me is new spiral-bound notebooks for the school year. But the minute Brett comes back in the door, it'll be a new car, a compact disc player, and Florida for winter vacation."

A sprinkler was getting the sidewalk wet in front of us and neither of us moved into the street, we just walked through it and got wet.

"I am completely sick of being a nice person," said my cousin Carolyn. "I feel like going out to puncture tires."

I giggled. "You know, you're not bad, Carolyn. Can I stay here all summer?"

"No. It's my turn to go somewhere. I get to go back to Vermont with you."

We began laughing crazily.

"The only hope," Carolyn confided, "is that Brett would have to be sorry enough to please my mother.

The apologies alone would take years. I don't think he'll do it."

We walked on in companionable sweatiness.

A car pulled up next to us. A car straight off one of the posters Joanna and I paper our room with. A 1963 maroon Cadillac convertible. It was packed with junior-high girls, and driven by a hugely overweight man. Everybody in it was laughing. "Carolyn Preffyn," they yelled, singsong. "Lyn Fyn! You forgot the party! You forgot the party!"

Carolyn clapped a hand over her mouth, doubled over almost to the grass, and burbled, "You're right! I forgot! Oh, Pammy, don't be mad. Can I still come? Please, please, please?"

"Why do you think we tracked you down?" said the fat man. "What's a party without my little girl's best friend?"

"Don't open the car doors," ordered one of the girls. "You have to climb in."

Carolyn clambered right over the sides of the Caddy and fell messily onto the laps of the other girls. Everybody shrieked and giggled and flung themselves around.

"You must be the cousin," said the fat man, grinning fatly.

I do not know why, but I am afraid of extremely fat people. There is something horrid about rolls of fat that I can't bear to look at, or be near. I didn't want to be in his car.

"Come on in," he said cheerfully, "join the crowd, we're on our way to the roller rink in Springfield, got the place reserved, plenty of games and cake and prizes."

I felt very old. That is not a feeling that comes over me often. The girls jammed seatbeltless into the beautiful convertible seemed like a younger, gigglier

110

set. Carolyn blended right in; she ceased to be my cousin and turned into just another silly girl.

"Come on, Shelley," Carolyn said. "It'll be fun. You'll love my friends."

"No, that's all right," I said quickly. "You go on. Have a great time. I'll see you later at home for Aunt Maggie's party."

"We won't be late," the fat man assured me. "I'm coming to that party myself. Went to school with your dad, you know. Yup. Graduated the year behind him."

"Mr. Hallahan, he won't even be there," said Carolyn, beating on the man's shoulders as if he were her property. "My mother didn't remember to tell the guest of honor to come on the right date."

Mr. Hallahan laughed hugely. "That's our boy Charlie," he said.

It seemed to me the better response would be "That's our girl Maggie." But I insisted Carolyn should go on without me, and finally they drove off.

I stood alone in Barrington. I was not exactly afraid, but I felt misplaced. Barrington was neither alien nor scary. But I was not part of it.

I walked slowly, as if expecting things to go wrong at each corner.

And things did.

How dumb daydreams can be!

I found myself facing the house Carolyn had pointed out—the one where Brett was staying with friends. I remembered it vividly because unlike most of the houses in the area, with big old shrubs and towering old trees, the foundation of this house had brand-new shrubs, about the size of footballs, looking fake and ridiculous.

I decided to knock on the door. Pleasant people—their name was Cameron, I remembered, the sort of loving, generous people who took in kids in trouble—would answer the bell, exclaiming, "Charlie's daughter!" Brett would say, "Gosh, I'm glad you came. I needed a cousin to escort me home and help me get along with my parents."

That was the daydream.

And I, the essential follower, the girl who likes Angus or Bev or Kimmie or Marley to lead the way, went alone up to a stranger's house to interfere with somebody else's life.

"Oh hi," said Brett without interest. "It's you."

Brett seemed so much older than I had expected. His tan was not golden like Toby's, but dark and hard. He wore shiny, reflective sunglasses that hid a third of his face. He glittered and yet I could not see him. I didn't feel related to him at all. There was nothing in him of the cousin I had played with in distant summers, the cousin who lowered his bike seat for me so I could ride it; the cousin who found Band-Aids for me when I scraped my knee; the cousin who gave me his ice-cream cone when I laughed so hard the ice cream fell out of mine and onto the sidewalk.

A tall, thin boy stared at me. Brett didn't introduce him. Miranda was there, motionless on the couch, staring at the TV. There were no adults around. The house had a thick, dead smell, as if ashtrays needed emptying, and sheets needed changing. All the shades had been pulled down, and the sun came through dully, hopelessly, into the sullen dark.

Who would run away from Aunt Maggie's sparkling, welcoming house to this?

Somebody either desperate or stupid.

"Whaddaya want?" said Brett.

"I just wanted to say hello," I said, completely flustered. "We haven't had a chance to see each other yet."

"Oh, wow, Brett, you're honored," said Miranda. "The cousin from New York City going out of her way for a little down-home chat."

The thin boy laughed. Miranda laughed. Brett remained behind his silver lenses.

"Are you coming to the party?" I said, feeling like a complete fool.

"Why would I want to hang out with that bunch of assholes?" said Brett.

The thin boy and Miranda laughed. The TV laughed, too, as if it were alive, and not merely spouting a laugh track.

The word shocked me. Not because I hadn't heard it plenty of times, but because it meant us: Grandma, Carolyn, Aunt Maggie, Uncle Todd, Angus, and *me*.

"Your own father can't be bothered to come and it's his party," said Brett. "What makes you think I'd go?"

No reasons came to mind.

"Aren't you supposed to be helping with the big party?" said Brett. "The big failure, I should say. Since as usual our sainted mother figured she could engineer everybody else's lives without asking first."

Poor Aunt Maggie! I thought. They're so mad at her.

But had we not been mad at her too, all these years since my parents divorced? Because Aunt Maggie went relentlessly on without faults or hard times?

Miranda began flicking a remote control. The television raced through channels, tossing scraps of conversation and bits of applause and music into the room like broken lives.

I was afraid of them.

This was what giving up looked like: shuttered and dusty and mean-mouthed.

I backed toward the door.

"Have a nice day," said Miranda.

I stumbled out the door. I closed it myself, because Brett didn't follow me toward the opening in that terrible place. I ran down the street, thankful for the shrubbery, for the short blocks, for the houses and garages and trees that hid me from whatever eyes might follow.

In all the hard times our family had had, nobody ever shut out the sun, or the world. Nobody ever hid like that. Nobody—except me.

I shut out my mother. Shut out her world. Hid from her.

I was half running now. The Barrington sun would have fried me like an egg if I had paused on the sidewalk. My hair turned sticky; even my thoughts stuck together.

I could not bear it! How could I be the one who was wrong?

They were the wrong ones!

I got dragged after them. I made none of the decisions, filed for none of the divorces.

I had come out on the main shopping street of Barrington.

The little mall where we got my new contacts was elsewhere; this was the quieter, old-fashioned end of town. A few of the storefronts were unoccupied, and a

114

lot of the parking places empty. The street had a summery feel, as if we were all waiting for something.

Years ago, my real mother had taken us for ice cream at a drugstore on this street when we visited. Was it still open? Could you still get an ice cream there?

I crossed the street. Not only was the drugstore still there, it still had a soda fountain.

Some things didn't change.

I felt safe from my terrible thoughts, from that dark, closed-up house, and the brutal sun. "I'll have a chocolate milk shake," I said, fishing in my jeans pocket for change. It cost less than in New York. I'd even have a few cents left.

I was aware of attention at one side. Of golden tan and long masculine arms and big masculine hands.

It was Toby.

Chapter 12

*H*ere's why I don't like to ask questions.

I'm *not* afraid of the answers.

I just don't think there should be any questions to start with. Your father should be your father; he should be married to your mother; you should all live happily ever after. And that's that.

"Hi, Shelley," said Toby eagerly.

He was as handsome as he had been yesterday afternoon.

"Let's sit in a booth," he said. "Come on." He took his butterscotch sundae and his cola, and my milk shake, and both our napkins and spoons, and nudged me toward a booth.

No boy ever had asked me to sit in a booth before.

Toby got straight to the point. Looking anxious, as though it really mattered, he said, "Does your father ever talk about me?" Then he dipped his spoon into his sundae and had an enormous, butterscotch-dripping mouthful of vanilla.

"I've always wanted to meet Charlie," said Toby, looking up from his ice cream and into my eyes. What was he looking for there? Blood ties? You wouldn't think, under the circumstances, that his attention could be evenly divided between the discussion topic and the food.

"I owe him a lot," Toby added.

I wanted to run. Like Angus. The whole way home to Vermont or New York City. I understood Angus, slamming doors, hiding out.

Families, divorce, and secrets are a lot like history-class discussions of "the bomb". Everybody gets extremely intense for forty-eight minutes, and says profound things, and considers the doom of mankind. But then the bell rings and you have more important things than the end of the world to consider, like whether or not you should lend your closest friend your silver-and-turquoise earrings.

Angus handed me this bomb a month ago, and when I thought about it, I was afraid and sweaty and angry.

But mostly, I didn't think about it.

You can't think about bombs.

Any more than you think about your own parents' divorce until it's there, and in your lap, which is filling with tears. I could use a bomb shelter right now, I thought. Because I think old Toby here is about to drop the bomb. "You owe him a lot?" I repeated, trying to be calm and ordinary. I paid very close attention to how I held my spoon. I kept control over the corners of my mouth, which were trying to tremble.

Like what was owed? Life? Breath?

Joanna and I had giggled and teased on the phone call when we considered a hidden half brother. She was rather thrilled by it. But it wasn't thrilling. It was sick and terrible.

Can I still love Daddy if he's really bad? I thought. If he couldn't be a father to Toby at all, then is he a good father? Even to me?

"If your father hadn't paid the bills," said Toby, "I don't know where we'd be now. I mean—"

Toby said "I mean" as if it were a whole sentence; as if nobody, including Toby, could possibly know what he meant.

"You read about terrible divorces and horrible betrayals," Toby said.

No. I didn't read about them. Who needed reading material on that when she could just live through it?

"And your father," said Toby.

The tears I was fighting were giving me a headache. Toby's technique of using little short phrases as if they were long explanations was making it hard to breathe.

"Well. He's *your* father," said Toby. "But he paid for me."

"Paid for you?" I echoed stupidly.

Toby looked at me oddly. "You mean—he really doesn't talk about me?" Toby stared down into his soda. He gave a funny little laugh. "I don't know whether to feel rotten about that or not."

"I feel pretty rotten," I said. I started crying into the chocolate milk shake. My tears dropped with surprising weight, not blending into the chocolate but lying in tiny teary puddles on top of the shake.

"Don't cry," whispered Toby, utterly appalled. "It's not your fault."

"I think it's terrible he never told us about you," I said.

118

"It's not that terrible," protested Toby.

"Not to tell us he has another son?"

Toby's jaw grew slack. Then he rolled his eyes. "Carolyn and Brett been getting back at you for all the times you conned them in New York? Shelley, your father isn't *my* father. I'm not *your* brother. The only son he has is Angus. Which from what I've heard about Angus is a darn good thing."

"You're not my brother?"

"How could I be your brother?"

"Angus said Daddy had a son named Toby."

"Oh, Angus probably overheard something, like half this dumb little gossipy town. My mother and your father hardly even got married before they separated. They were only sixteen, remember. Back then you had to quit high school if you were married, and so they weren't going to school and they weren't earning any money and the dishes got dirty and the car ran out of gas, and my mother went to live with her aunt in Chicago and your father hitchhiked to New York City. And they each went back to school and finished college and the funny thing was they stayed in love even though they couldn't stand living together or dealing with Barrington gossip. I mean, Shelley, you just can't imagine gossip in a small town. Me from Chicago and you from New York—we don't know gossip, not the way our parents do." He drank some Coke. "Celeste and Charlie were the focus of the whole town's attention, because she was the girl everybody had expected to go out and be a stunning female success, and your father was the boy who should have gone on to West Point or the presidency or something."

For just a minute I could see them: my father, when he was my age, golden and blurred in front of

119

Celeste's lovesick eyes; two kids, running away to find perfection and landing in pain. "Don't stop," I ordered him. "Tell me the rest."

"You never heard any of this?" He was amazed.

"Daddy never talks about Celeste. We only know about her from family gossip."

Toby nodded, but it was the kind of nod of somebody who doesn't understand. He *wanted* Daddy to have talked about it, I thought. Toby was sure he was special enough for Daddy to share him with us.

I stirred my tears into the chocolate shake and wondered if I would be able to taste the salt.

Perhaps there is no time when a secret is a good thing.

Perhaps for every person you protect, you damage another one. But who could know that? Who could weigh whether the protection or the exposure mattered more?

"They used to telephone each other whenever one of them had the money for the phone bill," said Toby, half laughing, as if he were abbreviating a beloved story he had heard a hundred times. "Your father. And my mother. They really didn't know what to do. My mother says they were afraid to meet each other again. Over the phone they could be kind and affectionate, because she was in Chicago and he was in New York. They were afraid if they both went to Barrington, or visited each other, or met in the middle, they'd fight again."

I tried to imagine them, hundreds of miles of telephone line between them, separate apartments and lives, but this time I couldn't do it, the images didn't appear; I could only see Daddy as the man I knew, a bear who laughed at everything and charged right on.

"I guess they were really just kids," Toby said dubiously.

I crossed Daddy and Angus in my mind. If I made Angus tall and older—locked into marriage, which was surely a lot scarier than a backyard bomb shelter—I could half see him.

I knew that Daddy had put himself through NYU nights while he was starting his own business. I knew that by the time I was born he was already a success. But I had not known he saved money for a phone call to the high school sweetheart who wore his ring but lived in another state.

"Well, they each fell in love again," said Toby finally. "Your father fell in love with your mother and my mother fell in love with my father. At that time they'd been apart for years. Their divorce made them sad. I think they felt instead of marrying other people they should have tried again." Toby looked at me with the narrow eyes of somebody seeing a thousand other things. "But they didn't want to try again."

"Just as well they didn't," I said. "We wouldn't exist."

Toby finished his sundae, and looked longingly at the bottom of the cup, as if hoping it would spontaneously regenerate a second helping. "Anyway, when I was very little, my father got killed in a car accident just after he had sunk every cent into a new business. There was nothing left. Absolutely nothing. And instead of turning to relatives in Barrington who would know all, tell all, and remember all for generations, my mother asked your father for money. She knew he had become very successful and she thought he would lend her a little, until she could figure out what to do."

I was starting to cry again. "And did he?"

121

Toby shook his head. "I can't believe you don't know this."

"Believe it. And tell me everything."

"He supported us until my mother finished law school. Three years. Mom says if it hadn't been for Charlie Wollcott, she would have been a typist instead of a lawyer and we'd still be on food stamps instead of taking vacations in Florida."

I knew that all my life I would remember the booth in the drugstore. The way Toby folded his napkin into a dinosaur. The way his hands looked: large, nervous hands, playing with paper and spoons to keep occupied. The way my hands looked: rigid, because I was afraid instead of playing with spoons I was going to grab his hands and hold them permanently.

"You going to have your milk shake or not?" Toby said. Boys can always concentrate on the important things. Like food.

"Not," I told him.

"How come?"

"I'm too nervous to swallow."

Toby thought about this. Nothing, including the final bomb and the doom of humanity, would ever stop a boy from eating.

I said, "You have it."

"You sure?"

"I'm sure. Just keep talking."

He was very obedient, was Toby. Aunt Maggie would not have approved of his table manners at all. He drank, spooned, and talked at the same time. It was a very chocolaty recital. "Your father, Shelley, sent us money for no reason except they'd loved each other once. He wrote that if they'd had a kid, he would have loved the kid, and he would love any child of hers, so he was glad to help."

Toby, the child my father had loved, was sitting across from me. Having my milk shake. I said, "Toby, I can't help it. I'm going to cry. A whole lot."

Toby looked very alarmed. "In here?"

"Or we could go outside."

"You can't stop yourself?"

"I don't have a delete-emotion button."

Toby grinned. "Sure you do. Everybody does. Come on. There's a rinky little traveling fair around the corner. I'll take you on the roller coaster."

"I hate roller coasters. If you think it's bad when I'm trying not to cry, meet me when I'm trying not to throw up."

"Nah, this is a rinky little roller coaster. For three-year-olds and their big five-year-old brothers." Toby stood up and took my hand. It was where my hand had wanted to be for an hour now.

Toby said, "Barrington somehow found out that your father was sending us child support all those years ago, and they figured it meant that I'm his kid, which I am not. You are, and Angus is, and what's her name is, but my father was named Richard Donnelly and I look like him and everything." Toby grinned, throwing in a little visual proof. Then he tightened his grip on my hand. Partly because we were crossing the street and partly for punctuation, to make his speeches stronger. "My mother says there isn't much in Barrington but corn, relatives, and rumors. So of course for the big reunion party, all Barrington's full of talk because I'm here at the same time with my grandparents, who were once your father's in-laws."

Outside, summer was as strong as hurricanes.

In New York, summer means gasping for breath, and hoping there will be no blackouts to knock out the

123

air-conditioning. In Vermont, summer means the lake, and the deep green trees, and quiet. But in Barrington, summer is a living thing: a burnished brilliance of sun and sky. A heat so great it lives on you and in you, ruling your health and your thoughts.

I wanted to embrace summer, if I could not embrace Toby. The heat was enough to bake away cares, to broil off worries.

Toby said, "I've always wanted to meet Charlie. When my mother talks about him, it's not the way anybody else talks about ex-husbands. She still loves him, I guess. Not getting-married-again love. But . . . well . . . love."

And here I had thought I wasn't going to cry.

I cried.

My tears trailed down my face and I had to tilt my head back to keep my contacts in place. The wind lifted my hair off my neck and threw grit on my tear tracks. "How old are you, anyway?" I said.

"Seventeen in three months. That's another thing. Your father was supporting us when he had two little kids already. You and your big sister. What's her name?"

Nobody had ever referred to Joanna as what's her name. "Joanna," I said. "I think Daddy's always had extra money."

"Listen, people can have a million extra and still not share a dime with their ex-wives."

Toby bought us entrance tickets. Fifty cents. It really was a rinky little fair. It had only six rides. I opted for a small-child ride. Toby paid a quarter for each of us and we climbed on merry-go-round horses: aqua with a white mane for me, and red with a black mane for Toby. We were the only people riding. The music wound itself up and slowly the horses began to circle. When Toby was up, I was down. We waved at each other, and our knees bumped.

All along, I never minded The Perfects, or anybody else, being Perfect as long as we had some Perfection too. I always had a better father than anybody; a father who was always there, and funny, and strong, and gave us bear hugs, and took us to the lake or the mountains or the movies and loved doing it.

Okay, so he has divorces and skips out on surprise parties, I thought. He's still Perfect. He never stopped being Perfect.

The booths held green teddy bears you could win by throwing darts or shooting air guns or tossing beanbags. They sold fried dough and cotton candy, foot-long hot dogs, corn dogs, and soft ice cream. They sold T-shirts with monster faces and tacky jewelry with misspelled names.

We did every single booth. "I hope we don't win anything," I said. "I don't know what I would do with a mirror that has a beer ad printed on it."

We rode the merry-go-round seven times, getting up and moving around until we had tried all the horses. Then we even rode the ducks put there for the two-year-olds.

I looked at my watch. Five o'clock in the afternoon.

Lenses drunk at eight, new contacts bought when the optometrist had them in stock at ten, home to call Joanna at eleven, Carolyn off to the roller rink by one, scorned by Brett at one-thirty, staring up at the Ferris wheel by three.

"Oh!" I said. "The party! I've got to get home."

I imagined my aunt Maggie doing all her wonderful preparations and here not only was Daddy not going to show—I was missing too!

125

I bet Aunt Maggie doesn't know about Daddy supporting Toby, I thought suddenly. How could she say the things she does about him if she knew that? She'd want Brett to be *exactly* like Daddy if she knew!

Why did Daddy keep it such a secret?

"Let's walk to your aunt's," said Toby. "Barrington people go straight from the house to the car. I always think it's so funny that people in the country never walk."

"We'll be city people together," I agreed, thinking, And all Barrington can gossip now wondering about us.

We left the fairgrounds. We had sidewalks all the way to Aunt Maggie's. Toby didn't take my hand. He talked about all kinds of stuff and I hardly heard any of it because I was so involved in an inner debate about whether *I* should take *his* hand.

The views were longer in Barrington than in Vermont. Trees in Vermont stalk the hillsides and meadows like vandals, filling every space. Beyond the edges of Barrington the horizon swooped a huge distance under blue armloads of sky, stretching to unknown farms and fields.

Hay had been cut. It was bleaching in the sun.

It smelled wonderful and safe.

"Do you think Brett will come home?" I interrupted him.

Toby didn't seem to mind the interruption. "Sure. Eventually. Brett is kind of ordinary, you know. It's tough being ordinary when your parents want you to be incredibly special."

We were the only people using the shaded sidewalks that lined every street. "I'm ordinary," I said.

Toby stared at me. *"You?"*

We crossed the final street. A block away you could tell that Aunt Maggie and Uncle Todd were having a huge party. Cars lined the road and were parked on lawns, and doubled in driveways. Wonderful meat-on-coals smells permeated the entire neighborhood.

"I've always sort of thought of you guys as relatives," said Toby, looking rather shy. "Do you mind?"

"I wasn't thinking of you as a cousin," I said.

"Well, I promise you I'm not your brother." Toby was grinning. His grin was nothing like my father's, nothing like DeWitt's, or anybody else's. It was all his, and I quivered, and wanted it to be mine, as if I could possess his grin, make it surface when I wanted it to, and wipe it off when I needed him to be serious. "Brother?" I repeated. "No. I was thinking of you as—"

No sunburn, even the worst degree, ever turned cheeks so red. I folded my arms across my chest. I looked away from Toby toward a couple getting out of their car. The husband was carrying a platter of double-chocolate brownies and the wife was balancing a lemon meringue pie. "Wow, look at all the food they're bringing," I babbled. "What a feast it's going to be. I really wish Daddy were going to be here tonight! He loves dessert. Are you staying long enough in Barrington to meet him? I don't even really know when he'll show up. Whenever his business is done, I guess."

A woman with a glass bowl of fresh strawberries and cream walked over the grass and into the backyard. The next couple carried a huge sheet cake and a sign that read WELCOME HOME CHARLIE!

Angus would eat that cake. He loved to eat icing. He always scraped away the best flowers and ribbons on the cake and left the insides for me.

"I'll see you around," said Toby.

"You're not—I mean—Oh, Toby, please come to the party. Be my guest."

Toby shook his head. I could not read his smile. It seemed uncertain, as if all the fears that he had taken away from me, he had been forced to keep for himself. He turned his head aside; in profile he was bony and very thin. When he turned back to face me, the thinness went away and he was handsome and nervous. It was like looking at two different people.

I wanted to get to know him. To find out whether his profile or his full face represented the real Toby, or whether, as with so many people, his features had nothing at all to do with his personality.

I did not want to join the party. I stood looking at him, and he at me, and whether he was thinking of fathers, I do not know, but I was drowning in a hundred thoughts that had nothing at all to do with parents. Thoughts that prickled through in trembly skin, flushed cheeks, shallow lungs.

Toby said, "Maybe tomorrow, Shelley? We could talk some more. Like—I could borrow my grandmother's car. We could go somewhere."

I nodded. "I'd like that."

Toby gave me a light kiss on the forehead, and walked away.

Chapter 13

"*W*here have you been?" hissed Carolyn. "My mother is furious. Your family does disappearing jobs like nobody else on earth." Carolyn bundled me up to her bedroom to get properly dressed. I was dusty and tear-streaked, so I hopped in the shower while she shouted through the crack in the bathroom door. "The white dress? The one with the little green sash?"

"No, I think the yellow two-piece dress, don't you?"

"No, it's too little-girl. Don't you want to look older, Shelley?"

"Okay, but I don't like the green sash."

"You can use my paisley belt, it's dark red and—"

"I hate paisley, it looks like pregnant worms."

Carolyn combed my wet hair and said it wasn't fair for some people to have great hair like mine, when people like her had to put up with crummy old ordinary hair.

I had always thought my hair was the crummy old ordinary hair.

Carolyn snorted.

I wore the yellow dress after all. It was very short and my tan was pretty nice by now. Carolyn loaned me cute little yellow sandals and a wonderful pair of earrings with tiny white, yellow, and blue beads that dangled all the way to my shoulders, like beading on Indian moccasins.

"I can't wear them," said Carolyn, shuddering. "They brush my cheek and I always think there are bugs landing on my skin. Now, where have you been all day?" Carolyn was wearing a bright red shirt, bright blue shorts, bright yellow belt, and bright green scarf. She looked like a crayon box. I couldn't decide if I liked all that color or not.

"Toby took me to the fair."

Carolyn dropped the hairbrush. *"Toby?"*

I nodded, trying to look casual, but failing because I was new at looking casual over boys.

Carolyn did not let me down. "Oh, Shelley, he's so cute. Isn't he the cutest person in this state? All right, why did he take you? Did he want to talk about family secrets or did he want to take you?"

"I don't know yet."

My cousin studied my face intently for lies. She didn't find any. "You have to tell me when you do know or I'll make your life miserable," said Carolyn. She braided three very narrow cornrows to keep my hair away from the right side of my face and let the earring show, and then she used a hot curler to make a banana curl on the other side for contrast. "I bet you and Joanna fix each other's hair all the time, huh?" said Carolyn longingly.

"No, mostly we just fix Joanna's hair."

130

"That rots," said Carolyn. "What good is a sister if you're just her servant?"

We talked about sisters and brothers and whether we had any use for them. "Guess what," she whispered. "Brett's coming home!"

"That's wonderful! How did it happen?"

"Mom and Dad went over to the house where he's staying and confronted the parents. Mr. and Mrs. Cameron agreed that by giving Brett a free home and free food and affection, they were aiding and abetting his running away. Like accessories to the crime, you know. So they gave Brett the ultimatum. He can't stay there another night." Carolyn was both delighted and angry about it. "He'll get his party," she said. "He'll slip in and start eating apple pie and Grandma will give him ten hundred hugs and we'll all pretend nothing has happened."

How different from my family!

Of course, we can't pretend. Mommy did cross the ocean to live with Jean-Paul. Daddy is married to Annette.

I said, "But how do you know Brett will come home? What if he just finds another friend to live with, or hitchhikes away?"

Carolyn gasped. It had not occurred to her there could be anything other than a happy ending to this. An easy ending.

"I'm mad at Brett," she said, "but I want things to be the same. I want him to come home. Right now."

I started to tell her that things are never the same, and coming home doesn't change things back. And then my own word echoed back to me. *Mommy*. I was calling her Mommy again.

Something in me had softened.

Joanna had been right. I was the one who was maddest of all. And I never even knew it. "Tell me that story again," I said. "The progidal one."

"Prodigal."

"What's that mean? Do you have a dictionary?"

"It means wasteful," said Carolyn, who explained to me that she had done more than her fair share of Sunday school; she had probably done my share as well, and frankly she was sick of the whole thing.

"Wasteful?" I repeated, remembering the story. "Of what?"

"His inheritance. His family's love and patience. Because he ran off and was bad and did drugs and slept around and gambled and all that."

"Did they do drugs in biblical days?"

"No, but you're supposed to update everything. Like instead of leprosy, now you say AIDS. Listen," said Carolyn, "I don't want to be a Sunday school teacher. Let's go have supper and fun."

So who was prodigal? I thought. Was I the one being wasteful of my family's love and patience, and now I've come back home to Mommy? Or was Mommy the one being wasteful and now I'm letting her come home to me?

We went downstairs to join the party. I loved my yellow dress. It did make me feel like a little girl, and yet also playful and older and pretty. Especially my hair felt great. Carolyn was excellent with hair.

"Once everybody found out the Major Character wasn't going to be here," explained Carolyn, "they said they were coming when they felt like it, because they didn't have to bother with the surprise element, so they're all here hours early and my mother is a wreck."

"I should think she'd be rejoicing because her party's going to be such a success even without Daddy."

"Not my mother," said Carolyn. "She likes things to follow her Master Plan."

I was only fourteen and nobody had followed my Master Plan yet.

I was right, I thought, Aunt Maggie is younger than I am!

People were bringing extra folding chairs, and wine, and liters of 7-Up, and cans of OFF! to fight the insects.

The back steps led straight into the yard, but there was also a little back stoop where you could stand up high, surveying the territory. Carolyn darted off into the grass to greet somebody who immediately shouted about how tall she had gotten. The most boring thing about reunions is that everybody has to comment on how tall you have gotten.

Angus was circulating. He had a notebook with him and was attacking each guest with pencil poised.

I didn't cringe.

I didn't want to abandon the party and I didn't want to break his pencil in half.

It was Angus's project, not mine. For the very first time in my life as his older sister, I didn't get all panicky that people would point to me and say, "she's related to him, she's probably weird too."

It came to me that I had been living through Angus for many, many months. Maybe since Mommy left. I had been letting Angus do anything that took daring, I had been laughing at Angus's antics instead of coming up with any of my own, and I had thought more about Angus so that I wouldn't have to think much about Shelley.

He has been the VCR of my life, I thought.

He's like a tape I play over and over instead of making my own film. Time to make my own film. Let Angus direct his movie, I'll direct mine.

My film. I would be beautiful, and always wear my hair dramatically, like this, with each side different, and wild earrings accentuating my long throat. Toby would be in the film, and fast cars, and dancing. Angus would not have a part. He was a little boy, only twelve, and I was going to be fifteen and wear my grandmother's engagement necklace to dances.

I—Shelley Wollcott—walked down the porch stairs, approached a pair of total strangers, and introduced myself. Lifetime first.

They were delighted to meet me. They were great fans of Charlie.

"Is that your brother over there?" said the man, laughing. "He's the kid with the toilet paper at the ball game, huh? I laughed so hard. He's been collecting autographs all over town today. Is he Charlie Wollcott's kid or what? Walks up to complete strangers—'Can I have your autograph?' And they say, 'But I'm nobody,' and the kid says, 'My father isn't. And he'll want everybody's autograph since he can't be here himself.' Bet he's got a hundred autographs in that notebook so far to give to Charlie."

"That's adorable," said the wife.

"Charlie probably pays the kid to be different," said the husband, laughing again.

I circulated.

The menu was barbecued ribs, baked potatoes with sour cream, corn on the cob, beefsteak tomatoes, and the largest salad bowl in the world, filled with tossed lettuce, cucumbers, and bright red radishes cut into petals like roses. But the dessert table had everybody moaning about his waist and his diet. Fluffy cakes and layered chocolaty things and pastries with cinnamon sugar on top.

"Do I have to eat any of the real food?" asked Angus. "Or can I just start with the desserts?" Angus was being passed from guest to guest like an appetizer, so they could all exclaim, "Oh, this has to be Charlie's son!"

They knew I was Charlie's daughter, and Annette was Charlie's wife, but they didn't get so excited about it as they did with Angus.

I sneaked one of those double-chocolate brownies and stood in the corner of the yard, where the edge of the yellow awning was brushed by the lowest branches of the great maple tree. In the setting sun I was just another gold-edged shadow.

A teasing voice said, "Now how many wives is this? Charlie's on what? Number five? Six?"

Aunt Maggie giggled, except she sounded like Joanna, and I jumped. "Sssshhhhh," said my aunt. "The children are very defensive. Don't let them hear you."

Somebody came up behind me and I knew it was Toby, he'd changed his mind, he couldn't wait till tomorrow, and I turned to hug Toby, to rejoice in his grin and his company—but it was Annette and Angus. Angus muttered, "Has anybody on earth really had five or six wives?"

"Henry the Eighth of England," said Annette. "He was always getting married again. Sometimes he divorced the old one but mostly he just cut off her head."

Angus was awestruck. "Why would anybody marry

135

him after that? I bet the girls would be nervous about marrying a guy that cut off three or four heads in a row."

Annette said that was one of the little mysteries of history.

Angus said as soon as the library was open he would look up Henry the Eighth. He flipped over to a fresh page in his autograph notebook. He would start a new list, he told us seriously. He would make a list of how many wives all the men in Barrington had had.

Annette said that perhaps Angus would like her to cut *his* head off.

I cheered this idea, but of course Aunt Maggie overheard and she was shocked to find Annette threatening death by axe blade.

"And of course I want you to meet Charlie's new wife, Annette," said Aunt Maggie, in just the tone of voice you would use if your brother married a potential murderer, "and his son, Angus, and his daughter Shelley. My other niece, Joanna, I'm sorry to say is in *France,* staying with the children's mother, it's one of these—" Aunt Maggie paused.

Broken families, I thought.

Annette flushed and Angus flipped to a new page in his notebook.

I wanted to talk back to Aunt Maggie. I bet you don't know that Daddy paid for Toby, I thought. I bet Daddy didn't trust you with the facts. Or else he forgot about you and didn't bother.

"And these are Joel and Beth Schmidt," Aunt Maggie finished the introductions. "Beth dated your father in high school."

"Pre-Celeste?" said Angus, interested.

Everybody laughed. "Very pre-Celeste," agreed Beth

Schmidt. I looked at her with fascination. She wore many rings on each hand, around which the flesh bulged with fat. Her hair was partly gray, and held down with bobby pins, and she was still pretending to be a size twelve, and wearing the dress she had bought when she was a size twelve, and she looked awful. If Daddy saw her, he would certainly rejoice in his decision to stop dating Beth.

Beth leaned back against Joel's equally large stomach. "We were such good friends with—well, with your real mother, Shelley. And of course I hope we'll be good friends with your, well, your, uh, stepmother, too." She smiled brightly.

For a minute I wanted to kick her in the shins.

But only for a minute.

No doubt about it; a man marries three times and it's awkward for the old friends and family. So I forgave the woman for not knowing how to tell me she had liked my mother.

But also, Aunt Maggie turned to this woman and said softly, "They have a hard time dealing with being a broken family. You have to be understanding."

Annette grabbed Angus's wrist, which was good, because sharp pencils can be as bad as axes.

Maybe people from stable families can be understanding. Maybe all those backyards must naturally make you understanding. I wouldn't know. I'm new to backyards. "We are not broken, Aunt Maggie. Plates get broken, glasses get broken, and legs get broken. Families do not get broken." Angus supplied the pantomime that we would be happy to break legs or plates. "And if anything is broken around here, it's *your* family," I said. "And you're too cowardly to admit it."

Aunt Maggie gasped.

137

Beth and Joel hastily said they thought they would just refill their drinks.

A long time ago, when we were driving up to Vermont, house hunting, a stone flicked up off the road and hit the windshield. At first there was just a hole, with a few little cuts radiating off it. But as we drove along, the cuts grew. Shattery lines tore across the glass, and linked up with each other, and slowly the entire windshield became a sea of glassy cracks. It didn't fall apart. But you couldn't see through it anymore.

That's how I shattered, I thought. When Mommy left Daddy to go with Jean-Paul, the cuts grew and connected until I was all one frosty collage of splinters.

We *were* broken, I realized, admitting it at last. But families must have very strong glue. I'd been repaired. Just this summer.

We stood there: Aunt Maggie, Annette, Angus, and me.

Aunt Maggie said, "You're right, Shelley. I'm sorry for saying that. I know I get overbearing. I guess that I'm still hoping that we haven't actually broken, Brett and I." Aunt Maggie gave a funny little sobbing laugh. She held out her arms to me.

For a long minute I stared at her empty arms. I could hardly tell whose they were—Aunt Maggie's . . . or my mother's.

I stepped inside the circle of her arms and she closed them around me and our hug was a rocking hug, a dancing hug.

"Maggie," called Uncle Todd from the back door. "The Ellisons are here!"

Aunt Maggie let go. She walked toward Uncle Todd, thickly, as if she were swimming.

"Guess what, Annette," I said, wanting to share it with her. My eyes were shining. It seemed that even my hair was glowing and my cheeks must have been red-hot with pleasure. "I'm going to visit Mommy after all, Annette. This very summer. What do you think? Isn't that great? My own mother?"

Annette burst into tears.

Chapter 14

*P*eople's emotions are always lying there, waiting for you to step on them and muddy them up and squash them beneath your feet.

"Annette, stop crying," I muttered, shoving her into the house, "people will see you, they'll think there's something wrong, they already don't understand about Daddy because of Toby, and Angus being weird."

"I thought you and I were getting along so well," wept Annette. "Who's Toby?"

"Toby isn't Daddy's son," I said. "And we *are* getting along so well. That's the whole point. So I'm calling her Mommy again."

Annette said if he didn't get here soon, she was going to have a complete and total nervous breakdown.

"If who doesn't get here soon? Toby?"

"Who is Toby? Why would I care about Toby? Your father. And what made you suddenly want to visit France? You won't even get on the phone with your mother."

"I know, but I'm the prodigal daughter. Or she's the prodigal mother. We're going to party, I can feel it. I'm ready."

Annette said, "I thought you were the stable one, Shelley. Are you starting a mental collapse, or well into it?"

"You thought I was the stable one?" I said.

Angus joined us. "Go away," I said to him.

"No. Why is Annette crying? Do you want to see my autograph collection?"

"Angus, did you ask anybody how many wives they've had?" I demanded.

"No, what do you think, I'm weird or something?"

Annette began laughing insanely.

"Don't laugh like that, Annette," said Angus. "People will think you're weird."

"People would be right," said Annette. She headed for the stairs, but a pack of guests who had just used the bathroom were coming down. She headed for the living room, but a pack of guests who were sick of the mosquitoes outside were entering it.

My grandmother emerged from the living room. The Preffyns had one of those houses where nobody ever uses the living room. They look in the door, as if they're at a historical house with velvet ropes to block passage, but they never actually go in.

"Annette, darling, come sit with me for a minute," said Grandma. "You look a little strung out."

We all went into the living room. Delicately, worrying because Aunt Maggie would be able to see our footprints on the nap of the carpet.

Grandma said she had been crying herself just a little bit. "People always cry a little bit at reunions," she said. "Like weddings. Or funerals. There's something very painful and very beautiful about your very own family."

Annette turned her face to the wall.

It's not her very own family, I thought. There's nothing beautiful here for her. All she has is trouble.

Annette turned back to face us again, and somehow she had gotten strength from checking out the wallpaper. Maybe we should take a roll home. "I'm just a little frazzled from the plane flight," she said. We let it pass.

Angus said he wanted to know what stable meant, anyhow. It seemed to be the most important word in Barrington conversations.

"It means you are not affected by change," said Grandma. "In physics, it means the atoms don't decay. They just go on and on, always the same."

"How boring!" said my brother. "And here I thought it was good to be stable. You mean all stable means is that every morning you wake up and there's nothing new? But I like change."

Grandma looked as if she wanted to take all three of us, one by one, onto her lap for snuggling, including Annette. Annette just looked as if she wanted the next flight out.

"Who's Toby, anyhow?" said Annette. "And what do you mean, he isn't Daddy's son?"

So I explained.

Angus, with the same amount of interest he had shown in Vermont, namely very little, said that was pretty nice of Dad, huh?

Annette said, yes, he's like that.

And I said, "But why was it a secret when it's so nice? I thought you only kept bad things secret."

"Barrington gave your father a pain in the neck, just the way it did Celeste," said Grandma, laughing. "Just the way it did me. Why do you think I went to Arizona? Everybody in Barrington always has to be *knowing* things."

Angus was fascinated at last. "You mean you lied when you said you moved because the winters are bad?"

"The winters are bad," said Grandma. "But eighty years in Barrington were enough. For your father, sixteen years in Barrington were enough. He liked to keep his life to himself. You can't do that in a small town."

Grandma forgave him, I thought. He ran away all those years ago, and had divorces, and troubles, and gave her grief, and she doesn't care. "Does Aunt Maggie know about Toby?" I said.

"We all know about Toby, he's spent every summer of his life here with his grandparents, and half of it on my front porch."

"Drinking lemonade." I nodded, envying Toby.

"But I doubt very much if Maggie knew your father supported Toby and Celeste for several years. Your father didn't think it was anybody's business. I don't think he'd consider it a secret, just something in the past that's between him and Celeste." Grandma looked very soft and sad.

"Are you crying, Grandma?" I said.

"Yes, honey. I'm very proud of your father."

"He's pretty great, huh, Annette?" Angus said.

Annette shrugged.

"Just because you have to party without him," said Angus, "is no reason to get mad at him."

"She's crying because I'm going to visit Mommy after all," I said. "But how come, Annette? Why aren't you glad?"

She shrugged.

"Love isn't flat, like a freshly ironed sheet, Shelley," said my grandmother. But it was Annette's hand that her gnarled fingers touched. "Love is a tangle, hair that's never been brushed."

Annette said, "I thought I was more important. I guess in spite of all my best intentions about keeping my perspective, I decided I came first."

Angus explained to her that stepmothers never came first.

Annette tilted her head back to keep the tears from coming out. "I know," she said.

"But you come second," Angus told her.

Out in the yard we heard a tremendous hullabaloo. People were shouting, yelling, and cheering.

"What's that?" said Angus, obviously hoping for a fire or an explosion to liven things up. He leaped up, grateful for an excuse to abandon all these emotional women cluttering up the place, and raced out.

Grandma stood up and took my arm for support. "Might as well see what all the commotion is about," she said.

Annette followed us without enthusiasm, as if any commotion Barrington might rustle up was assuredly not going to be worth the trip.

We walked out the back door.

"Surprise!" shouted my father.

He stood at the edge of the yard, tall and heavy and laughing. He shouted out the names of all his old friends, and yelled hello to his sister Maggie, and bellowed with joy at the sight of the dessert table.

144

Angus threw himself on Daddy. "You fibbed," said Angus. "You said you weren't coming for days."

"Are you kidding? Ruin your aunt Maggie's surprise party? I just had to add a little extra excitement to it."

"You were coming all along?" cried Angus joyfully. "You were just giving your own sister a hard time? Like a real brother and sister?" He and Daddy laughed, and socked each other.

Grandma and Aunt Maggie and I stared at each other.

"I don't know whether to beat him black-and-blue or join in the hugging," said Aunt Maggie.

"A person feels that way about brothers," I agreed.

Grandma began laughing. It was the soft, possessive love of people who had always known what Daddy was like, but now they knew again.

"Annette, did you know all along?" I said to her.

She rolled her eyes. "Of course. He thought it was funny."

What a pain for her! Listening to Aunt Maggie carry on. She could have given Daddy away. I bet she wanted to. But she stuck on his side even though he was being as much of a pain as Angus ever is.

Aunt Maggie began to laugh. I had thought she would never start laughing again in this world. "Charlie," she said to him, "I don't know how yet, but you're going to pay."

The guests all egged her on, with a dozen suggestions of what could be done to my father. Angus whipped out his notebook and wrote them all down.

I wanted to race up like Angus and fling myself on top of Daddy and be his special girl again. But I didn't.

Annette wanted to do the same thing. But she didn't. It was like opening the door for somebody, where you each step back and wait for the other person to go first, to be courteous.

Daddy is first for both of us, I thought.

And we don't know how to share very well. And Joanna can't share at all.

But it was his mother, my grandmother, that Daddy kissed first, and swung on his arm. Then he put one arm around Annette and one around me and hugged us both, crushingly. Even Daddy's one-armed hugs are bear hugs. "Daddy, you made us suffer. We had to listen to Aunt Maggie say bad things about you."

Daddy roared with laughter.

I didn't have to protect him, I thought. Daddy never cared what anybody here thought. Only *I* cared!

Carolyn came over for her hug, but she was shy about it. My father is so much more energetic than her father. Daddy shook hands with Uncle Todd and then finally he said, "Maggie. Don't be mad. I had to do it to you. The situation begged for it."

Maggie heaved a huge sigh. Several people began singing "For She's a Jolly Good Fellow." Maggie allowed my father to kiss her cheek. She called him some names, and people with videos told her to talk louder, and people with cameras immortalized the Wollcott clan.

Grandma, Daddy, Annette, me, Angus, Uncle Todd, Aunt Maggie, and Carolyn, all hugging.

"Your son has a present for you," said Aunt Maggie. "Autographs of everybody in town." She moved into the shadows, letting my father have the stage he was so good at taking over anyway, and I saw Uncle Todd put his arm around my aunt. Brett, I thought. The photograph will remind them, forever and ever, that one summer they were missing a son.

Angus displayed his collection proudly. He looked at the gathering of relatives with satisfaction. "We're all here now," he said contentedly, and left us, because a latecomer had brought different food.

The party changed.

Laughter was longer and louder, the way laughter always is when my father is there, and the stories funnier and the food yummier. The heat did not lessen, but nobody went into the air-conditioning now; everyone gathered around my father, and told stories, and shouted out punch lines, and passed drinks and barbecue and extra napkins.

Angus's sentence hit me.

"We're all here now."

But we weren't all here. Joanna, our sister, she wasn't here. Mother, our real mother, she wasn't here. All my family reunions will be partial, I thought.

I wondered what my wedding would be like. Extra pews for extra families. Double-length invitations to list all the parents.

How many divorces are we going to have? I thought. You can't divorce sisters, can you?

How had Joanna fallen out of the bottom of our family like this?

Oh, Jo, come quick, get here quick, we need you!

Carolyn said, "Shelley, there's another long-distance call for you."

I practically fainted. Was that ESP or what?

"It's a boy," said Carolyn.

Long-distance? Could Toby have gone all the way back to Chicago by now? But—

147

There is no privacy in other people's houses. You can't say to your hostess, "Get out of your own room, I want to take the call alone." So Carolyn ran up the stairs with me, and into her room with me, and jumped on her bed with me, and leaned down to pick up her phone with me, and sat with her yellow hair one inch away from the receiver.

"Hello?" I said.

"Hi. It's DeWitt."

"DeWitt! How did you find me? Is everything all right? What's going on? Why are you calling?" I was laughing and shaking and whipping the phone cord around.

"I just wanted to say hi. And see how it was going. And if Annette sagged, and Joanna came, and Toby turned out to be your brother."

"Oh, DeWitt, you wouldn't believe it. Toby's not my brother, but he is the son of Daddy's first wife. He's really nice. I met him. We went to the fair." I could see DeWitt, his shaggy hair, the face that had too much forehead until his smile equaled it out, like an equation in math. "DeWitt, how did you know where to call me?" I could see him more clearly right now, in Carolyn's room, than I had see him the whole month he was rowing me around his lake.

"I asked the Frankels. They have your number there in case of emergency."

We giggled breathlessly. I said, "How was the hike?"

"It was good. I held up best. I was strongest. We didn't meet anything scary though. No bears. And guess what. The Lake Association hired me to paint docks for the rest of the summer so I'll be here when you get back after all."

148

"Oh, DeWitt, that's so neat! I can't wait to see you. I've only been here two days and my whole life has changed. I'll help you paint. We'll talk."

DeWitt told me more about the hike and I told him more about my family and then somebody at DeWitt's end reminded him it was a toll call and he had to hang up. "Bye," said DeWitt hesitantly, as if he had something else to say.

"Bye. I—I'll see you in a few days, then." I shivered with the honor of the call. "DeWitt? I'm really glad you called me."

"Hey, yeah. Great." said DeWitt.

I hung up. I stared at the telephone as if it were as special as the necklace Grandma gave me.

"Was that your boyfriend?" Carolyn burst out. "You didn't tell me you have a boyfriend. I can't believe you've been here all this time and you didn't tell me all about your boyfriend."

All this time.

I had been in Barrington two days.

"Why didn't you?" demanded Carolyn.

I felt my age. I felt fourteen going on fifteen, I felt the summer before my freshman year, I felt *me*. The cousin from New York City. The cool one, who knew what she was doing.

I shrugged. I didn't want to say I hadn't mentioned my boyfriend because I hadn't known he was one. "I guess we hadn't gotten to that yet," I said. "You know. We would have. Later."

Carolyn sighed happily. "It was too intimate to talk about until you knew me better, huh? Will you tell me absolutely everything later on?" She leaned forward, and stared into my eyes in a meaningful way. "I want to know how, Shelley."

149

I kind of wanted to know how, myself. I didn't think a description of DeWitt's hands on my knees was what Carolyn had in mind.

We floated back out into the party. DeWitt had actually gone to the trouble of getting my number from the Frankels, and getting permission to make the long-distance call, all because he wanted to be sure I knew that he'd be at the lake after all. I would have a reunion with DeWitt.

Carolyn was floating along for other reasons. She thought I was going to tell her all about sex. I had a good book to recommend to her, but it was back in New York.

The party was over.

The guests had gone home.

It was three in the morning.

Angus had fallen asleep in the grass and Daddy maneuvered him back to bed. Grandma had hardly stayed up at all after Daddy arrived. I couldn't imagine being tired just when the party really took off, but Grandma said when you were eighty, you were even tired for parties.

Carolyn and I had huge black plastic garbage bags we were dragging around the yard, stuffing in used paper napkins, paper cups, paper plates, and plastic spoons. Annette was covering miles of uneaten spareribs in plastic wrap, and Daddy was having an argument with Aunt Maggie.

"Why are you mad at me?" he said. "I thought it was funny. I swore Annette to secrecy and didn't even let Angus and Shelley in on the joke."

Aunt Maggie was crying.

"It was the best party ever," protested my father.

Aunt Maggie kept on crying.

"Okay, I'm sorry," said my father. "It was juvenile, it was dumb, I admit it, but that's the kind of family we always were, Maggie. I was always getting into trouble and you were always having to handle it, and I figured that it would be like old times and you'd laugh and—"

"You are such a conceited person, Charlie Wollcott. If you think I have time to worry about your inconsiderate, stupid pranks, you are wrong. I am worried about my son. The Camerons told him to leave and he did. But he didn't come home! He's not here. He could be anywhere! Chicago. New York. Hitchhiking, getting picked up by mass murderers or rapists of young boys. And you're playing games."

Uncle Todd sighed. "Maggie, you're getting melodramatic. I'm sure Brett just went to another friend's house. He's very popular, you know. He has plenty of friends. After he wears out his welcome at one place, he can just move on to another."

"That's even worse!" cried Aunt Maggie. "There won't be a street in town where I can drive, wondering if my own son is living there."

"In the morning we'll find him," said Uncle Todd.

"You're not even worried about him!" shrieked Aunt Maggie.

"I'm worried about us," said Uncle Todd. "I'm worried about putting this family back together. But no, I'm not worried about Brett. He's not going to do anything foolish like vanish across the horizon, Maggie. He has another Little League game tomorrow and he has to be at work by eight. I'll just go down to the warehouse in the morning and have a talk with him."

Aunt Maggie stared at the vast tray of leftover foods Annette was preparing to squeeze into the refrigerator. "This was supposed to be such a wonderful week. I planned all spring about having an anniversary celebration and welcome-home parties and a family reunion—but it's *my* family that isn't together."

Annette and I hung our heads. We had actually wanted something like this to happen to them, so they wouldn't be Perfect anymore.

Chapter 15

My letter to Joanna the next day was the second-longest thing I had ever written. The longest was last year's term paper on the origins of the Korean War, which I may say did not interest me then, does not interest me now, and had a grade that exactly matched my lack of interest. Still, it was long, and I thought that the teacher should at least have given me credit for length.

I knew Joanna would give me credit for length.

. . . so Daddy comforted Annette that she is still very important, and was probably the major cause in my coming to terms with Mommy and Jean-Paul, and that Annette being so stable is probably the most vital part of our family right now. Annette liked that and luckily Angus didn't argue. I could have, but I didn't. You have to give Annette another chance, Joanna. She really is very decent. And then I told Daddy and Annette how DeWitt had telephoned and wants me to go out with him once I'm back in Vermont. And Annette told Daddy about the engagement necklace Grandma gave me and how we're going to shop for a really special dress to go with it and Daddy said maybe I would be going to that dance with DeWitt, and Angus said that if DeWitt and I got married and had a son we had to make a solemn promise not to name our innocent kid DeWitt because there was such a thing as going too far.

I stopped writing the letter.

What was Grandma going to give Joanna? Joanna was the oldest grandchild and the first granddaughter. I had gotten such a special gift—but was there something left for Joanna? Grandma couldn't have left Joanna out, could she? Was there a family rule that if you didn't come to the reunion you didn't get a good present? Would Grandma send Joanna a pair of socks?

"Who you writing to, sugar?" said my father, coming up behind me and kissing my hair eleven times. He has never outgrown kissing us, and Angus now has to keep furniture between himself and Daddy so Daddy can't get all maudlin and kissy on him.

"Joanna. I'm telling her about the necklace and the party and how I'm going to France now, too, and DeWitt telephoning and all."

"I knew when you finally took off it would be like a volcano," said Daddy, "but I didn't think it would happen over two days when I was away."

I looked at him almost shyly. "I haven't told you about the real explosion."

Daddy hit his head in mock horror. "Are you taking Angus's slot in life now, Shelley? You're going to be the one to start things?"

I nodded.

"Well, whatever it is, you look pretty thrilled about it. Tell me."

"I have a date this afternoon. We're just going for a drive. Daddy, it's Toby. Celeste's Toby. He's a wonderful person. We got started talking because I hadn't understood the gossip and I was afraid of—well, don't laugh, but Angus and I sort of thought Toby might be *your* son but of course it turned out—"

"Celeste's Toby?" repeated my father. He looked thunderstruck. (I have never understood that. It's lightning that strikes you. My father looked lightningstruck.) "Wait a minute, Shelley," he said, almost gasping for breath. "You have a date with—with—"

"With Toby. Celeste's son from her second marriage. And he wants to meet you, Daddy."

"I'm not ready for this," said my father.

"Okay. You can meet him another time. He's coming for me at two."

"No. You can't go for a drive with—I mean, Shelley, I know what happens when—well, when Celeste and I went for drives, we—"

I said, "I hardly know Toby. All we're going to do is drive."

"One thing leads to another."

"Not that fast, Daddy. Don't look so sick. He is a great person."

My father really did look sick. He said, "I don't want you making all the mistakes I did. This is a little close to home. My daughter dating the son of my first wife? Shelley, no."

I felt stiff and angry.

My father moaned dramatically. "All my life I've coped with Joanna and with Angus, and before them with your mother and before her, Celeste. But you— Shelley, you're my easy one. My stable one."

"I hate that word stable."

"Well, I know a person gets a little tired of it, but still—"

"I hate being counted on!" I said. "I want to be the one who does stuff you don't expect. I had chemistry. You know what a stabilizer is? It keeps a mixture from being changed by new additions. I'm sick of being a stabilizer."

My father said, "I don't see anything good coming out of this."

"Daddy! You were nice to Toby! You paid to take care of him when he was little and Celeste was trying to go to law school! You were wonderful to him. And he came out a wonderful person. And he asked me to go out with him. So there."

Actually I wasn't sure if this was a date or not. It was perfectly possible that Toby just wanted to talk of family and pasts in more detail.

My father frowned. "How do you know that? I have never discussed it with anybody."

"Toby told me. How come you never discussed it? Aren't you proud of it? Daddy, I'm proud of it. I'm proud of you."

. . . and then, Joanna, Daddy began telling me about Sunday school. I guess they are really into Sunday school around here. Or they were in Daddy's day. He said you're not supposed to let your right hand know what your left hand is

156

doing. I said what on earth does that mean? If your right hand doesn't know that your left hand is turning the steering wheel, there's going to be an accident. Daddy said real charity does not brag, even to itself. He said when you're doing a kindness, boasting ruins it. (I still don't see where the hands come in.)

So I said how come you never took us to Sunday school if you learned so much there? He said when he left Barrington, he *really* left Barrington, and that included things like Sunday school that symbolized Barrington.

"You don't like Barrington, do you?" I said. I had thought Daddy saw Barrington as I did, with front porches and lemonade and hugs, a time of summer and happiness.

"I'm starting to like Barrington again, honey," he said. "I went through a long, heavy-duty rebellion. It lasted for years. I didn't really want a reunion. Not that I wasn't glad to get together with my family again, but I didn't much want to remember Barrington again."

"But everybody was so glad to see you, Daddy! You were the star of the show."

Daddy laughed. "It's tough growing up, Shelley. Have you noticed?"

"Yes," I said emphatically.

"I had a tough time. Takes most people a couple of years. Took me a couple of decades. Nobody really wants to go back and stand where he was jeered at and mocked when he was a kid."

"What did they jeer at you for?"

"Celeste. Dropping out of school, being a failure, getting married at sixteen, bringing embarrassment and rage to our families, going on welfare—"

"Daddy! You were on welfare?"

"Just for a little while. Celeste and I had absolutely no idea how to be grown-ups. So we gave up. She went to live with her aunt in Chicago so her aunt could be the grown-up and I went to New York and lived with a bunch of young guys and didn't make the slightest attempt to be a grown-up."

. . . we talked for hours, Joanna. I love hearing stories about when Daddy was little. Of course, he wasn't little then; he was a teenager; but he makes himself sound so little. And *dumb*. I mean, with every single story, you want to go, Daddy, how could you have done so many things wrong in such a short time?

Anyway, he didn't want me to go out with Toby. But he didn't want to refuse me, either, so he let me go. But he wouldn't meet Toby. He said life was emotional enough without that.

It's five of two, Joanna.
And Toby's due.

Chapter 16

"*M*y grandparents want to meet you," said Toby.

"Why?" I said cautiously.

"Because if your father had stayed married to my mother, which is what they all wanted, you'd be their granddaughter."

"Genes don't work that way," I objected. "I'd be somebody else." We had just driven around. Toby loved driving. He certainly seemed to be good at it. He didn't fit into Miranda's description of Brett, that was for sure. We drove all over the countryside, he gripping the wheel, and me over by my window. We had talked mothers and fathers for hours. I was ready to talk boys and girls, but Toby gave no sign of tiring of the parental subject. "Anyway, I thought people didn't want Celeste and Charlie to get married."

"Well, they didn't want them to get married at sixteen," agreed Toby. "But other than that, it was fine."

Toby and I laughed so hard he could hardly drive.

"We're going to get killed," he gasped. He pulled over onto the shoulder of the highway and we sat in the dust clouds and laughed and laughed.

"You know, only people like us really know how to laugh," said Toby. "I dated this girl who was another Perfect, like your aunt Maggie's family, you know, and she took everything so seriously."

"Poor Aunt Maggie," I said. "She's so broken up about Brett."

"I don't blame her. Brett is being a jerk. But you know, sometimes I think in families where nothing has ever gone wrong, when even the littlest thing does go wrong, they collapse. Brett always came in first, you know what I mean? He was the kind of kid that made a hole in one the first time he swung a golf club. So he gets behind the wheel of a car, and he's a terrible driver, and what boy can admit he's a terrible driver? So Brett keeps on driving and has accidents and almost hits people and his father takes away the car and what happens? Brett's so mad that he didn't make a hole in one, he won't even come home again. He's just being a spoiled brat. Don't worry about him."

"Okay," I said cheerfully. I figured I had so many other worthwhile people to worry about anyhow, why give Brett worrying space? Let Miranda worry about Brett.

"Listen," said Toby.

Then he didn't say anything more.

We both giggled. I hadn't been around an older boy who still giggled. "I'm listening, okay?" I said.

"I'm not ready to talk yet though."

"Okay, then I won't listen."

We laughed insanely.

Toby said, "My mother is a basket case. I phoned

160

her to say I asked you out and she said, 'Charlie's daughter?'"

We couldn't stop laughing. Toby had tears running down his cheeks. I was wearing a huge oversize T-shirt so I used the bottom hem to mop his face and Toby said, "My mother is convinced you and I are going to run away to Chicago and get married."

"Nah. I won't be sixteen until next year."

"When's your birthday?"

"November."

"Rats. We'll have to postpone it."

. . . I know, I know, this letter is eleven pages long already, Joanna. Look at it as practice. You want to teach school, and this can be a paper you're correcting. Anyway, I hardly ever had such a good time. I don't really know what was so funny, Joanna. Toby's mother decided (five minutes after being told he was taking me out; is that a coincidence?) that he needed to be back in Chicago with her after all and help out. Help out how? I asked Toby and he said, help her not worry that I'm going to make the same mistakes she did. I said grown-ups must be obsessive about that, because all Aunt Maggie could say was that Brett was making the same mistakes my father had.

That sounds like Perfect, said Toby, *she* didn't have any mistakes in *her* past Brett could possibly repeat. And then a really funny thing happened, Jo. We were both ready to say good-bye. Good-bye for good. There really was something odd between us. We shared Daddy; shared a past; shared secrets. He *was* like a cousin or a brother.

I'm crazy about Toby—and yet . . . and yet
. . . Plus of course I have DeWitt waiting for
me out on the lake. I guess it's always easier to
do anything when somebody is waiting for
you. . . .

Toby kissed me good-bye. It was a real kiss. A boy-loves-girl kiss. I had never had one before.

In one soft touch of my lips to his, I knew why Daddy ran away with Celeste and why Daddy and Celeste were afraid to have Toby and me in the same car.

I wanted to kiss like that all my life, and yet . . . and yet . . .

I was ready to say good-bye.

"Next summer?" said Toby. "Will you visit again next summer?"

I nodded. I didn't want to speak. I wanted my lips to remember the kiss. He was very flushed. He turned the air-conditioning in the car up higher and drove me back home.

Home.

Aunt Maggie and Uncle Todd's, really.

And yet there is something about relatives that makes their house your house. It was home. It didn't have the wide front porch or the lemonade, but it had family.

"This is only my third day in Barrington," I said. "It feels like my third year."

Toby laughed. "I've always felt that way about this town. It's so slow. Nothing ever happens."

That was completely the opposite of what I was thinking. It seemed to me that more had happened in Barrington than happened in most lifetimes. I felt as if

I had shot right through my father's adolescence as well as grown through three or four years of my own. We pulled up in front of Aunt Maggie's, but Toby didn't turn into the driveway. "Bye," I whispered.

He sat on his side of the front seat, looking neither left nor right, as if he did not intend to look at my face again. "Bye."

I was hurt, and then I saw the gathering only a few feet away in the driveway. Grandma, Aunt Maggie, Annette, and Daddy were all getting ready to go somewhere.

"You want to meet Daddy?" I whispered.

"Not with that audience."

"I don't blame you. I'll hop out. You can drive away and pretend you didn't see them."

Toby swallowed. "Okay. Bye. Go."

I opened my door.

But it didn't work that easily. What ever does? My father left the group, walked over to Toby's car, and came around to the driver's side. "Hello, Toby," he said, bending over and putting out his right hand. "I've always wanted to meet you."

I finished getting out.

My father said, "I gather it's been a pretty emotional weekend here, Toby. I don't want you to be left with any questions or worries. So how about you and I go have a hamburger somewhere and talk? Or would that upset your mother?"

Toby shrugged the way Angus used to when he was very little, not because he didn't care, but because words were too much for him.

My father got into the passenger seat, right where I had been, and told me he'd be back in an hour or so and why didn't I go shopping with the girls?

. . . so, Joanna, the really unfair part is that
none of us know what Daddy and Toby talked
about. I mean, of course I *do* know, I know
they talked about Celeste and Daddy's marriage,
and divorce, and why he helped her out with
Toby all those years ago. But I didn't get to be
there, to hear the exact words, and put in my
two cents' worth, and see if they touched each
other. If Daddy, who hugs us all the time, also
hugged Toby. As if Toby could have been his
son, and maybe, in a tiny, distant way, *is* his
son.

We went shopping instead. Antiquing, actually. There were all these shops in a little village near Barrington, filled with dusty old stuff
that Annette kept saying would look perfect at
the summer house and Aunt Maggie kept
saying were far too high-priced and Grandma
kept saying she used to have when she was a
little girl. I was megabored. And yet my head
was crammed full of thoughts, tumbling and
whirling like clothes in a dryer. . . .

"Are you going back to work, Annette?" I said.
"Did you decide?"

Annette nodded. "Yes. I am. I really loved it, you
know. And I'm good at it. It's nice to do things you're
really good at."

I fingered the back of the old kitchen chair Annette said she would buy if we had come by car and
had any way to get it home again. It looked like a
perfectly ordinary chair to me, not worth toting a couple thousand yards, let alone miles.

"Will that bother you?" said Annette.

164

We were eye level. Annette is exactly my height. We could share clothes, I thought suddenly.

The world seemed full of things I had not yet shared with Annette. "Yes," I said. "It was fun with you home. In Vermont."

When we drove home, Angus was walking toward us down the sidewalk. He didn't recognize the car so he didn't change his manner even when we slowed down.

Angus was wearing a hot-pink T-shirt that he had cut into shreds, so that pink ribbons blew around his chest. He had on baggy orange-and-scarlet shorts. Carolyn had braided string bracelets in purple and black around his wrists and Angus had not let her cut the ends off, so his wrists dripped cords. He had slashed the toes open on his high-top black sneakers. Probably they were too small for him already, even though Annette had just bought them when school ended. The sneakers flapped open like mouths with sock tongues and he was dancing in order to make them flap more. He had his leg slung over his shoulder and every time he hopped the leg kicked him in the behind.

"How do you live with that?" Aunt Maggie said to Annette quite seriously.

Annette said that she was getting used to it.

I said that I would never get used to it.

Aunt Maggie said she thought she would probably be on my team. She began a long story about how my father used to humiliate her back when they were about ten and twelve. Grandma kept adding details and correcting Aunt Maggie—"No, it was on Elm Street, not Maple, darling, remember—in front of the Bergers' house?"

Carolyn and I changed into our swimsuits and

swam in the backyard pool instead of going to the town pool because she said she didn't want to run into Brett or Miranda. That seemed reasonable to me. Annette said that it was fine with her if Carolyn spent the rest of the summer with us and I said, "Except whatever week I go to France." Carolyn said she thought she would go to France with me too, and Aunt Maggie said she thought not.

Angus lit the charcoal fire for Uncle Todd while Aunt Maggie put on water to boil for cooking the corn on the cob that Grandma had bought at the farmers' market.

I said, "Could we squeeze lemons?"

Grandma said she thought she could remember how to cut a lemon in half, so we made lemonade.

It was a family reunion.

Complete. Perfect.

Everybody but Brett. Daddy said that not all family reunions happened when you wanted them to. That Brett might be home in an hour or a year. I said, "Can't we help?" and Daddy said no, because he had spent a good deal of his life telling his Barrington relations to butt out of his child-rearing decisions and he could hardly butt into this one. Anyway, said Daddy, Uncle Todd and Brett were doing just fine together. Uncle Todd was taking Brett out for breakfast every morning. Which naturally just made Aunt Maggie feel ten times worse. It was her demand for Perfection that was driving Brett crazy. Things weren't as bad as they seemed.

"I don't want you to worry, so I'm letting you in on it, Shelley," said my father. "The fact is that sometimes fathers and sons have to settle things alone, without the women." He looked at me rather sadly. "And some-

166

times mothers and daughters do too," he said. "I'm glad you're going to France."

"What if it doesn't work, Daddy? What if I'm still mad at Mommy?"

"It's only a week. Go see the Eiffel Tower instead of your mother then. But I think it will work. I think you're both ready."

"Are you still mad at Mommy?" I said.

My father was silent for a long time. "Honey, I can go back into the past and be mad at the sixteen-year-old boy who wouldn't do the dishes and threw the plates against the wall instead and made a sixteen-year-old girl so mad she went to live with her aunt. I can go back into the past and be mad at your mother for finding somebody more elegant and worldly and exciting than I am. But I love the family I have now. I love the people that you and Joanna and Angus have grown up to be. I love Annette. So mostly, no, I'm not mad. And I don't want you to be either, honey. Being mad takes up so much time. It's hard to be yourself when you're furious all the time. You weren't yourself, you know. You lived through Angus and through Joanna, but never through yourself. This weekend"—my father hugged me as hard as he ever had; so tight I could hardly breathe—"Shelley, you're here. It's my reunion with *you* this weekend."

Chapter 17

*T*he plane was delayed, of course.

Whenever you're eager to move on to the next phase of your life, the plane is always delayed.

We waited in the terminal as if we were waiting for the dentist. Endless silent staring at the bucket seats opposite, at other people's knees and the backs of their newspapers.

Carolyn sat very stiffly, so nobody would realize she had only flown twice before in her life. Daddy had bought her a guidebook to New York but she had hidden it so nobody would think she was a tourist, or dumb. (Angus had given her explicit instructions on how seasoned travelers traveled, to which Grandma said, "I think we can tell Angus is about to turn thirteen.")

Daddy bought two newspapers.

Annette began humming softly to herself.

Angus looked horrified. "Annette. Sssshhhh. People can hear you."

"Angus, I have quite a nice hum. I'm on pitch and everything."

Angus looked edgily around at the other waiting passengers. "People will think you're weird," he said in a low voice.

There was a long silence. Daddy and Annette and I stared at him.

I said, "Angus, are you embarrassed in public? Is Annette humiliating you with her weird behavior?"

"Yes."

Annette and I smiled at each other. I said, "Angus, this is the happiest day of my life. Revenge is at hand."

Angus looked wary.

"It is my turn," I said. "You've been the weird one for twelve years. I have stored up a bunch of public humiliation. I am going to stand up on this chair, Angus, and sing opera at the top of my lungs, while holding the leg and using it for a submachine gun. Airline personnel will arrest me for causing a riot, and you will be embarrassed to death."

Angus believed me, of course, because two weeks earlier he would have done the same thing, and loved every minute of it. "I—I have to go to the bathroom," whispered Angus weakly, and he fled before I made a spectacle of myself.

My stepmother, my father, my cousin, and I laughed the entire hour until the plane was called.

A Selected List of Fiction from Mammoth

While every effort is made to keep prices low, it is sometimes necessary to increase prices at short notice. Mandarin Paperbacks reserves the right to show new retail prices on covers which may differ from those previously advertised in the text or elsewhere.

The prices shown below were correct at the time of going to press.

☑	7497 0847 6	**The Face on the Milk Carton**	Caroline B Cooney	£3.99
☑	7497 0343 1	**The Stone Menagerie**	Anne Fine	£3.99
☑	7497 2304 1	**Shadow Man**	Cynthia D Grant	£3.99
☑	7497 2651 2	**Creepers**	Keith Gray	£3.99
☑	7497 2641 5	**Heart to Heart**	Miriam Hodgson (editor)	£3.99
☑	7497 1793 9	**Ten Hours To Live**	Pete Johnson	£4.50
☑	7497 0281 8	**The Homeward Bounders**	Diana Wynne Jones	£4.50
☑	7497 1707 6	**Who'll Catch the Nightmares?**	Linda Kempton	£3.99
☑	7497 1061 6	**A Little Love Song**	Michelle Magorian	£4.99
☑	7497 1482 4	**Writing in Martian**	Andrew Matthews	£2.99
☑	7497 0323 7	**Silver**	Norma Fox Mazer	£3.99
☑	7497 1699 1	**You Just Don't Listen!**	Sam McBratney	£3.50
☑	7497 1685 1	**The Boy in the Bubble**	Ian Strachan	£3.99
☑	7497 0009 2	**Secret Diary of Adrian Mole**	Sue Townsend	£4.50
☑	7497 0333 4	**Plague 99**	Jean Ure	£3.99
☑	7497 2617 2	**Secrets**	Sue Welford	£3.99
☑	7497 0147 1	**A Walk on the Wild Side**	Robert Westall	£3.50

All these books are available at your bookshop or newsagent, or can be ordered direct from the address below. Just tick the titles you want and fill in the form below.

Cash Sales Department, PO Box 5, Rushden, Northants NN10 6YX.
Fax: 01933 414047 : Phone: 01933 414000.

Please send cheque, payable to 'Reed Book Services Ltd.', or postal order for purchase price quoted and allow the following for postage and packing:

£1.00 for the first book, 50p for the second; FREE POSTAGE AND PACKING FOR THREE BOOKS OR MORE PER ORDER.

NAME (Block letters) .... Philip ....

ADDRESS ..... 50 Almond Road ....

...... Dunfermline ....

☐ I enclose my remittance for ... 2 weeks ....

☐ I wish to pay by Access/Visa Card Number ☐☐☐☐☐☐☐☐☐☐☐☐☐☐☐☐

Expiry Date ☐☐☐☐

Signature ..... W. Philip. ....

Please quote our reference: MAND